WEST END BRANCH
11 x 5/14
27 x 4/19
D0011460
WITHDRAWN

Who's Who

Katani Summers
a.k.a. Kgirl ... Katani has a strong fashion sense and business savvy. She is stylish, loyal & cool.

Avery Madden
Avery is passionate about all sports and animal rights. She is energetic, optimistic & outspoken.

Charlotte Ramsey
A self-acknowledged "klutz" and an aspiring writer, Charlotte is all too familiar with being the new kid in town. She is intelligent, worldly & curious.

Isabel Martinez
Her ambition is to be an artist. She was the last to join the Beacon Street Girls. She is artistic, sensitive & kind.

Maeve Kaplan-Taylor
Maeve wants to be a movie star. Bubbly and upbeat, she wears her heart on her sleeve. She is entertaining, friendly & fun.

Ms. Razzberry Pink
The stylishly pink proprietor of the "Think Pink" boutique is chic, gracious & charming.

Marty
The adopted best dog friend of the Beacon Street Girls is feisty, cuddly & suave.

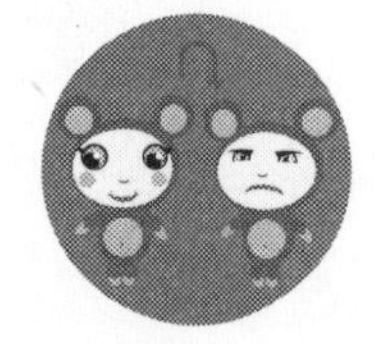

Happy Lucky Thingy and alter ego **Mad Nasty Thingy**
Marty's favorite chew toy, it is known to reveal its alter ego when shaken too roughly. He is most often happy.

Be sure to read all of our books:

BOOK 1 - worst enemies/best friends

BOOK 2 - bad news/good news

BOOK 3 - letters from the heart

BOOK 4 - out of bounds

BOOK 5 - promises, promises

BOOK 6 - lake rescue

Coming soon:

BOOK 8 - lucky charm - June '06

BOOK 9 - fashion frenzy - Sep '06

BSG Special Adventure Book - Fall '06

charlotte in paris

Alameda Free Library
1550 Oak Street
Alameda, CA 94501

Copyright © 2006 by B*tween Productions, Inc.,
Home of the Beacon Street Girls.
Beacon Street Girls, Kgirl, B*tween Productions, B*Street, and the characters Maeve, Avery, Charlotte, Isabel, Katani, Marty, Nick, Anna, Joline, and Happy Lucky Thingy
are registered trademarks and/or copyrights of B*tween Productions, Inc.

All rights reserved. No part of this book may be reproduced in any form or by any electronic or mechanical means, including information storage and retrieval systems, without permission in writing from the publisher, except by a reviewer who may quote brief passages in a review. If you purchased this book without a cover, you should be aware that this book is stolen property. It was reported as "unsold and destroyed" to the publisher, and neither the author nor the publisher has received any payment for this "stripped book."

First Edition

Special thanks to Dr. John Knight, Associate Professor of Pediatrics at Harvard Medical School and Director of the Center for Adolescent Substance Abuse Research at Children's Hospital Boston. Dr. Knight conducts scientific studies on the early identification and treatment of alcohol and drug problems in teenagers funded by the National Institute on Alcohol Abuse and Alcoholism, the National Institute on Drug Abuse, the Substance Abuse and Mental Health Services Administration, and the Robert Wood Johnson Foundation. He is a fellow of the American Academy of Pediatrics.

The characters and events in this book are fictitious.
Any similarity to real persons, living or dead, is coincidental and not intended by the author. References to real people, events, establishments, organizations, products, or locales are intended only to provide a sense of authenticity, and are not to be construed as endorsements.

Series Editor: Roberta MacPhee
Art Direction: Pamela M. Esty
Book Design: Dina Barsky
Illustration: Pamela M. Esty
Cover photograph: Digital composition

Produced by B*tween Productions, Inc.
1666 Massachusetts Avenue, Suite 17
Lexington, MA 02420

ISBN: 0-9758511-7-9

CIP data is available at the Library of Congress
10 9 8 7 6 5 4 3 2

Printed in Canada

Visit the Beacon Street Girls at beaconstreetgirls.com

freaked out

PART ONE

HAWAII OR BUST

"I think we'd better sit this party out."
party time!
Isabel M.

CHAPTER 1

INVITATION TO TROUBLE

IT WAS ONLY third period. But Maeve could tell that her least favorite person in the whole world, Mr. Sherman, was about to ruin a perfectly good day. It all began with his snarky, "Good morning, class. I hope you had a fun weekend, since you will surely want to spend this week studying." Maeve was convinced that the teacher everyone secretly called "the Crow"was looking directly at her when he made the announcement.

"Why would we want to do that?" Dillon Johnson whispered to Maeve. Neither she nor Dillon was the greatest math student in the world. Dillon would totally rather have fun than study, and Maeve had decided a long time ago that math was just about the hardest thing in the world to figure out. Whoever invented the stuff anyway? she wondered, as she twirled a stray red curl that refused to stay behind her ear no matter how many times she placed it there.

"Mr. S, I can't study this week. It would interfere with my chess playing," Pete Wexler announced, sitting up straight at his desk (something he never did). Everyone knew he was faking it. Pete Wexler had never even seen a chess board. He spent all his time on the soccer field or the basketball court. Chess was for nerds, according to Pete.

"Be quiet, Pete, I want ..." Before Lisa Chen, the best math student in level C, could finish her sentence, the door opened and in skidded Henry Yurt, late pass in hand. The Yurtmeister was sporting an enormous green Dr. Seuss hat. Everyone snickered as Mr. Sherman raced to snatch the hat off the Yurtmeister's head. But Henry, too nimble for the Crow, ducked, slipped, and tumbled down the aisle, arms and legs akimbo.

The class erupted in raucous laughter. Mr. Sherman rapped on the desk with his ruler, but no one was listening. The Yurtmeister was the star of the show. Maybe, she thought, I should tell Henry to take acting with me. He's such a scene stealer.

"Yurtster, you are one brave man," Pete Wexler said in admiration as he watched Henry Yurt jump to his feet.

"Thank you, thank you," bowed the Yurtmeister.

"Mr. Yurt, or should I say, *Thing One*, please take your seat, I have had enough of your antics for today." Mr. Sherman's reference to *Thing One* from *The Cat in the Hat* and Henry's solemn face broke everyone up all over again. Even Maeve, who was still waiting anxiously for the rest of Mr. Sherman's announcement, chuckled.

Maeve nibbled on her fingernail. A whole week of studying could potentially ruin her plans. Plus, it meant the unthinkable was coming. The thing that made Maeve chew her nails and want to curl up on her bed with her comforter covering everything but the tip of her nose. The nightmare on Beacon Street ... M A T H T E S T!

She glanced over at Isabel, who was still smiling at the

Yurtmeister's antics, which included twirling his Seuss hat on his arm. Suddenly, true to his name, the Crow swooped in and snatched the ridiculous green monstrosity out of the air before the Yurtmeister could grab it.

"Playtime is over, ladies and gentlemen," Mr. Sherman smirked, obviously pleased with his capture.

"Do you think Mr. Sherman is immature or something?" Maeve whispered to Avery who was sitting behind her.

"Duh, do you think?" Avery responded. "Look at him. He thinks he just won the state b-ball championships."

Maeve turned and gave her friend a quick smile. Everything was sports with Avery.

"Eyes front, Ms. Taylor-Kaplan."

Maeve blushed. The Crow loved to embarrass kids, but did he have to get her name wrong?

Suddenly, there was a knock on the door. The head of the math department waved at Mr. Sherman to step outside. The Crow warned the class to stay focused. On what, Maeve wasn't quite sure.

Two seats away, Joline Kaminsky, chief whisperer and assistant to the chief Queen of Mean, Anna McMasters, turned to give Maeve her perfected "You are so uncool and dweebish" look.

When Joline turned her back on Maeve, Dillon blew a spit ball at the back of her head. Joline spun around so fast that she looked like an alien out of a *Star Wars* movie.

"Wow, Joline," goofed Josh Trentini. "Can you do that maneuver again? My uncle is in special effects in Hollywood. I bet he could use you as a model."

"Oh, your uncle must be George Lucas 'cause you look just like Chewbacca," Joline shot back. Avery had to laugh. Joline was so quick with her comebacks. But as she gave a sidelong glance at Josh, she realized he really did kind of look like Chewbacca. He was tall for his age and big, plus his hair was long and bushy. Josh looked angry, but Avery knew from years of teasing from her two big brothers that you better not dish it out if you can't take getting something back. Josh would have to learn that. But she did feel sorry for him. His cheeks were bright red.

In a flash, the Yurtmeister was on his feet.

"My fellow citizens. We must stop these ridiculous behaviors." Leaning over, he grabbed his green hat off the desk, threw it into the air and bobbed and weaved so that he was able to catch it perfectly on his head. The boys in the back clapped and whistled, but Lisa Chen was annoyed.

"You want double homework, Henry?" she scolded. "You're going to get us all in trouble."

Everyone quieted down. Double math homework was too awful to imagine. A sheepish Henry slunk back to his seat. Getting everyone in trouble wouldn't win the class president any votes in the next election.

Flipping her curls over her shoulder, Maeve gave Dillon her best red carpet smile. It was so awfully nice of him to blow a spit ball at Joline in her defense. Dillon could be so dashing sometimes. Perhaps, she fantasized, he really was a prince in disguise.

Unnerved by Maeve's megawatt smile, Dillon slumped back in his chair and promptly fell over onto the floor. Maeve shrugged. Perhaps dashing was not quite the right word to describe Dillon.

When he heard the crash, Mr. Sherman marched back into the room and began rapping on his desk with his ruler. "Order in the classroom," he cawed.

Maeve glanced around to see if she could catch Isabel's

eye. She wished that Isabel would look over and see that her desperate friend was in need of an Isabel smile.

Mr. Sherman raised his black brow and turned his dark eyes toward the class. *Something wicked this way comes,* Maeve shuddered, remembering a scary movie by that title that she had snuck into her dad's movie theater to watch. "Now that Mr. Yurt has finished his Oscar-worthy performance …"

Whistles arose from the class but they were immediately quelled by Mr. Sherman's dancing unibrow—the big black thing that really did make him look like a crow ready to swoop down on unsuspecting prey. "As I was saying," he glanced around the class, making certain students, like Maeve, Isabel, and a short kid with freckles who always sat in the back, squirm in their seats. "You must plan your time carefully this week."

This time Maeve was positive that he was specifically referring to her. After all, she reasoned, she was the worst math student in the class, maybe even the whole school. Perhaps, they would put her in *People* magazine for being the worst seventh-grade math student in the entire United States of America.

"Spill it, man," a boy in the back suddenly hissed.

"Who said that?" The Crow spun around but no one would look at him or answer. Major unwritten rule at Abigail Adams Junior High: Never "rat" on a fellow student in class.

"Every one of you needs to pass the mid-term math test I'm giving you on Friday. The test will cover everything you've learned so far this year." The Crow paused, wrinkled his brow, and for effect added, "Just think how much fun we're all going to have." This time he looked directly at Maeve.

Everyone saw it. Isabel gave her a little half smile that said, "I feel your pain." There was something so comforting about hanging out with Isabel, thought Maeve. She had a knack for making everyone feel like that just because you couldn't do something well didn't mean you were stupid or anything. Maeve was glad that Isabel had moved from Detroit and was now one of the Beacon Street Girls.

As the Crow paced back and forth spouting something about math being a thing of beauty, Maeve wondered whether all math teachers were this weird. She shivered even though the room was warm and she had on her favorite pink velvet hoodie—the one Ms. Razzberry Pink had told her was all the rage in New York City.

Out of the blue, Maeve's breath started to come in little spurts. It finally sank in. A test—a huge math test. The worst, evilest, nastiest, most stomachache-giving thing in the whole wide world was looming before her.

Well, what if she didn't pass the test? Maeve contemplated. Would that be so bad? After all, she was Maeve Kaplan-Taylor, nodding to her fans on the red carpet, Oscar in hand. Who needs mathematics? She raised her head imperiously. What 12 year old was supposed to remember what she'd learned a month ago or two weeks ago, anyway?

Maeve looked around the room. Everyone else was writing things down in their notebooks about what was going to be on the test. Gosh, what had she missed? She glanced over at the clock. Hopefully the bell would ring before the Crow could pounce and ask her a question. He was going row by row now, forcing kids to come to the board and solve a problem. Her absolute worst fear.

All of a sudden, Mr. Sherman appeared in front of her.

"Ms. Taylor-Kaplan …"

Maeve gulped. How did he get here that fast? Why did he always get her name wrong? He was two rows back the last time she looked. "If you feel you need extra help, see me after class. We'll talk it over."

"I'll be glad to help her," smirked Joline.

"Better get a backup, Maeve," quipped Avery.

Maeve glared back at Joline. She might be horrible in math, but she wasn't going to let the likes of Joline Kaminsky get the better of her.

"Maeve." Mr. Sherman was growing impatient.

Maeve raised her eyes and smiled sweetly at the Crow. Like she would ever ask a bird of prey for help. Thank goodness for Matt, she thought as she nodded at the teacher. The tutor her parents had hired was really nice and worked hard to explain everything. She just wished she was better at math to begin with.

Clang went the bell. She was saved. Maeve leapt out of her seat and bolted toward the door. She couldn't wait to get to the cafeteria.

"Maeve, you look funny. What's the matter?" asked Katani, who was waiting outside for her friends. Katani was a math whiz and in level A, which was right next door to C. Josh said the teachers didn't call them A or C levels because all the parents would get bent out of shape. Nobody wanted their kid in level C; like their child would have self-esteem problems or something. But the kids knew the real deal, and most of them didn't care, or like Maeve and Josh, pretended not to care.

"Mr. Sherman," Avery jumped to answer for Maeve. "He announced the big, huge mid-term and made it sound like we were all gonna go back to kindergarten if we don't pass it. Maevey here is freaking out," Avery teased.

As the girls started walking toward the cafeteria, the usually talkative Maeve remained quiet. Her stomach was going crazy and her palms were sweating. "Don't worry,

Maeve. I'll help you. This stuff is pretty easy once you get the hang of it," a confident Katani said. Maeve gave her a weak smile. Easy for you to say, she thought. You've got a math brain and I don't.

"Maeve, don't get all tied up in knots about this," Isabel interjected. "You only have to get a C to pass. You can do that," she said, giving Maeve a friendly pat on the shoulder. Maeve felt a little better. Isabel was right. She didn't have to be a superstar here. She just had to pass.

"Avery," Ms. Rodriguez called, catching up to them. "I know you're starving but could I see you for a few minutes about your book report?"

Avery looked a little worried but turned and limped back to Ms. Rodriguez's classroom.

"Avery is lucky," Charlotte said, joining the group.

"Yeah," said Katani. "It's amazing that she didn't break her ankle or even pull any ligaments when she fell at Lake Rescue. The doctor said if Avery would keep it tightly wrapped for a week or two, it should be good as new."

"I don't know what Avery would do if she couldn't play soccer or basketball, or whatever sport is coming up next. She'd probably explode," Isabel added.

Isabel was wearing a new blouse her grandmother in Mexico had embroidered for her. Katani stopped to admire it as they got to their lockers. As she struggled to unload her English book and grab the one for social studies, Katani's books and papers slid. Everything dropped on the floor. It was such an an uncharacteristic move for the always in control Kgirl that both girls began to laugh.

Charlotte bent over to help scoop things up. "That's my trick, Katani. I hope clumsiness isn't catching."

"I think she did that because she was watching Pete

Wexler walk by," Maeve teased.

"Oh, Maeve," Katani protested. "Who has time to even think about anything this week, let alone boys?"

"Is everyone up for a sleepover in the Tower Friday night?" Charlotte continued. "We've missed so many lately."

"Did you talk to Nick yesterday?" Maeve asked.

"I don't talk to Nick every day," Charlotte sounded bothered. "Besides, I am all talked out. My dad wanted to hear every single detail about Lake Rescue. I think he misses going on adventures."

"I can understand that," Katani sympathized. "Your dad is used to traveling all over the world and now he doesn't really get to go anywhere anymore. He is probably bored."

Charlotte felt a sudden stab of guilt. She was the one who had asked her dad to forego a job in England and stay here so she could go to Abigail Adams Junior High. She had always wanted a real home, a place to put down roots and have the same friends for a long time. Now she had the Beacon Street Girls—Maeve, Avery, Katani, and Isabel—as her best friends. They all lived near each other. They went to Montoya's for hot chocolate together. They had sleepovers. It was heaven, a dream come true for Charlotte. But what if it wasn't heaven for her dad? What if he was bored and wanted to go travel down the Amazon and she was stopping him?

"Charlotte, are you listening to me?" asked an impatient Maeve. "I had to baby-sit Sam all weekend. And I hardly saw my parents." Maeve pulled the wheelie that held her book bag and her laptop. "But at least they're talking to each other."

"That's a good sign," Charlotte said.

"Do you think?" Maeve hoped Charlotte was right.

ଊ

✿

The cafeteria was the usual beehive of activity. Anna and Joline were holding court with Kiki Underwood and a few eighth-grade boys in the corner. The BSG made their way across the room. Lunch with Anna and Joline and Empress Kiki was not on their menu. They plopped down their backpacks to mark their seats and rushed to get in line before it got too crowded.

Back at the table Isabel asked, "Where's Avery? She's been talking to Ms. Rodriguez for a long time now." She unwrapped the sandwich that was on the lunch menu and stared at it.

Maeve bit into her sandwich. "This sandwich needs serious help, Izzy. Better smother it with mustard, or it will feel like you're eating white cardboard." Isabel looked askance at her soggy white bread. She had high standards for food. Her family, and particularly her sister Elena Maria, was a group of fabulous cooks.

Katani straightened her sweater, which just happened to be the color of Maeve's mustard. "If Avery has to write it over again, you should help her, Charlotte. You're a good editor."

"Maybe we should have some study sessions together to make sure we pull through all the mid-terms we have," Isabel suggested. "Charlotte can help us with writing assignments, Katani can help us study math, and—"

"Do makeup and help us decorate a new blouse," Maeve smiled. "We can each buy a plain T-shirt, bring paint that won't wash out, and make matching tops. I think that sounds like much more fun than studying."

"I've been thinking about creating a modern art T-shirt." Katani scribbled a design on her napkin.

"I know, we could put washable paint on Marty's paws, then let him walk all over the shirts." Charlotte laughed at her own absurd idea. "Then we could paint them over with fabric paint." Charlotte loved brainstorming ideas with her friends.

"Avery will want to make lots of paw-print shirts and sell them to benefit the animal shelter," Charlotte commented.

Isabel thought that over and then added, "You know, that is kind of a cool idea for a fundraiser."

"Kind of a 'going-to-the-dogs' sale!" Charlotte joked.

The girls got so caught up in plans for new clothes that didn't cost a ton of money that they almost missed the event of the day.

"Is that Julie Faber coming toward us?" Isabel asked, poking Maeve with her elbow. "What's she handing out?"

"I can't believe it. I am so excited. I think that she's going to give us invitations to her party," gushed Maeve.

Charlotte and the BSG watched the skinny, dark-haired girl in the stylish jeans and pink velour zip-up head toward their table. Julie's party had been the talk in the halls for weeks. The BSG had figured that they weren't invited because they hadn't yet received invitations in the mail.

"A party!" Maeve clapped her hands. "Wonderful. Just what I need to get me out of math boot camp."

Julie carefully handed each Beacon Street Girl a pink envelope. She smiled and made a big production of it all, as if they were invitations to the Oscars. "One for you, Charlotte. One for you, Maeve, and one for you, Katani."

Maeve held the invitation to her nose. It smelled like fruit.

"Here's yours, Isabel. Love your T-shirt."

Attention flew away from the boring lunch sandwiches and centered on the sound of ripping paper.

"Oh, yay, the invitation says no presents," Isabel read. "That's a relief, since my allowance this week is stretched beyond belief."

"Hey, this is so sweet." Maeve shook the card. A Hawaiian

✿

girl wearing a grass skirt and a lei wiggled on the front of the invitation.

"Must be a Hawaiian birthday theme," Katani said with a crooked smile.

"You think?" Maeve giggled. "It's a week from Saturday. Maybe I'll be over getting grounded by then."

"You're grounded?" Isabel asked. "But we just got home from Lake Rescue—what have you done?"

"Nothing yet." Maeve looked very glum despite the idea of a party.

"What are you planning to do to get grounded?" Charlotte grinned.

"Come on, Charlotte. It's no secret. I'm going to flunk Friday's math test."

"How do you know?" Katani asked.

"Don't say that, Maeve," Charlotte pleaded. "If you think you're going to fail, you might really flunk the test."

Maeve nodded. "I am going to flunk, I'm going to flunk seventh grade even. When you guys move on, I'll still be stuck with Ms. Rodriguez, writing about my worst fear or my most embarrassing moment, which I will be living out."

Maeve put her arm across her forehead and swooned like a character in a movie. She was so dramatic, her friends broke into a hysterical frenzy.

"Oh, Maeve, we're not laughing because you're worried about the test," Isabel said. "I'm worried about it, too. But what makes you think that they will keep you back?"

"My mind just keeps going there, and I can't seem to stop it. It kind of goes like this ..."

Aloha!
Party Time

Oh, baby you don't have a mind for math
It's too hard and wanna take a nap
All those numbers and my brain is whack
Gonna get dumped and sacked
Oh, baby, don't have a mind for math.

Maeve's math rap produced a burst of hilarity from all the BSG. Maeve's brain on math might be "whack," but everyone agreed with Charlotte when she said, "Maeve, forget math, your other talents are prodigious!"

Maeve grinned at her friends and then made her Hawaiian dancer wiggle. "Are we supposed to wear costumes? Like maybe, grass skirts?"

"How about our matching pajamas?" Isabel's eyes twinkled, reminding everyone how the BSG's prison pajamas had won Henry Yurt's Pajama Day contest's most creative award. "They'd look good with leis. I'm going to get a hula hoop and start practicing."

"I bet I can find my old one," Maeve said. "My mother read once that wiggling inside a hula hoop might improve my reading. Some weird brain thing. So I became a whiz at hula hooping, but I still couldn't read. That was before we discovered that I couldn't process what I was reading and I wrote a bunch of letters backwards."

"You could write all your sentences using palindromes," Charlotte said, giving up on her sandwich and nibbling pickle slices and carrots.

"What's a palinmacallit?" Maeve asked.

"You know, a word that is the same spelled backwards or forwards. The classic example is *Madam, I'm Adam.*"

"How about, *a Toyota*." Isabel laughed. "That's fun."

"Like Anna." Katani nodded toward where Anna and

Joline were cackling with the table of boys next to them. "Don't you think Anna and Joline sound like a pair of hens at feeding time?"

"A real pair of quacks if you ask me," offered Charlotte.

"Charlotte Ramsey," scolded Maeve. "That's so unlike you, and really, really funny."

"I wonder what boys Julie invited to the party," Charlotte said, wanting to get off the subject of Anna and Joline. The Queens of Mean made her uncomfortable. Charlotte never wanted to be a target of their meanness, but neither did she want to duck and hide.

"Don't you mean you hope she invited Nick Montoya?" Isabel teased.

"I didn't exactly mean Nick," Charlotte laughed. "I just meant, well, you know—"

"We know. Nick. Who else would you mean?" Maeve teased. "Personally, I hope she invited Dillon. He is such a good dancer."

"Don't look now, but isn't that Nick and Dillon heading right for our table? Should Katani and I leave?" Isabel stood up. But the big smile on her face said she was teasing, and that no way was she leaving. She liked Nick, too, even though she knew he was Charlotte's not-so-secret main crush.

Maeve pulled her down. "Don't even consider it, Izzy."

"Yeah, sit down, Isabel," Charlotte said.

I just gotta pass that math test, Maeve crossed her fingers behind her back. I can't miss the "party of the year."

Both boys had gotten a wiggling hula girl invitation too. They waved them in the air, then sat down at the BSG table to make plans.

"I heard we all have to wear grass skirts," Dillon said.

"Boys, too?" Charlotte asked.

✿

Maeve shook her head. "I've seen every movie ever made in a place where they wear grass skirts. I think you should wear Hawaiian shirts. You can get them at a secondhand store."

"No way am I wearing a grass skirt," Nick smiled at Charlotte. Charlotte thought Nick would look very handsome in a Hawaiian shirt.

"Me either." Isabel high-fived Nick.

"Maybe Julie's parents will hire a Hawaiian band. Is there any Hawaiian hip hop music, Maeve?" Katani asked.

"Don't think I've heard of any Hawaiian hip hop groups."

Dillon asked Maeve if she would dance with him at the party. Maeve nodded. Dillon was a really good dancer. Not as good as Tim Cole, her hip hop partner, of course, but very respectable. At that moment the music from *South Pacific* popped into her head. She stared dreamily at Dillon, imagining the two of them dancing under a waterfall with Hawaiian drums pounding in the background.

When the bell signaled the end of lunch hour, the BSG began to disperse. As Maeve searched in her "backpack of shame" for her science notebook, her spirits lifted. She remembered that she was going to hip hop class after school. Just thinking about dancing made her feel better about life. After all, Snoopy said it best: "To dance is to live." Or was it, "To live is to dance"? Maeve shook her head. She always did that—got confused about the order of things. Maybe that was her problem with math, she mused.

CHAPTER 2

ᘓ

DECISIONS, DECISIONS

HIP HOP CLASS

"THANKS, DAD, for picking me up." Maeve jumped into her dad's car after school and reached across to give him a hug. It was too far to walk to class, and if she took the bus, she might be late. She didn't want to miss one minute of the highlight of her week. And, she didn't get to see her dad every day since her parents separated, and she missed him.

"No problem," he said. "I'll swing back in an hour. My new assistant at the theater is great, so I don't have to worry about being there every second of the day."

Maeve was so excited to get to class, she burst into the classroom, tossed her jacket onto a chair near the CD player, then looked around to see if Tim Cole, the best dancer in the class, was there. He wasn't, so she busied herself looking through Ms. Bennet's vintage hip hop collection. The teacher said she liked the older music better than today's artists.

Ms. Bennet had CDs all the way back to Ice-T and Salt-N-Pepa, the first major female hip hop group. Maeve, who didn't much like the gangsta rap, either, preferred some of

✿

these older artists, too.

"Hi, Maeve. Workin' on some requests?"

Maeve swung around to find herself standing way too close to Tim. She couldn't believe he'd sought her out to talk to. Tim Cole was in eighth grade and had even danced professionally for a music video. Everyone thought he was the coolest thing ever. He looked like a rock star in training with his gorgeous blonde hair and big blue eyes.

"Yeah, sort of. I like looking at the old CD covers, too."

Just as things were about to get awkward between them, Ms. Bennet walked in. Maeve knew that Tim was just being friendly. But he was so totally adorable, he made her nervous.

Nikki Bennet's class was awesome. Ms. Bennet had danced a lot of places professionally, but unfortunately, a series of ankle injuries had sidelined her indefinitely. Maeve thought about Isabel, who had wanted to be a dancer. It must be hard to get hurt and not know if you'll ever dance again. Maeve didn't know how old Ms. Bennet was, but she knew her town was lucky to have her teaching a hip hop class at the rec center.

"OK, dancers. Take your places. Warm up by yourself," Ms. Bennet clapped her hands. "Get those legs moving and grooving." She waved everybody into place.

Maeve had no trouble getting her legs moving. Who could stand still? She ignored everyone around her, forgot school, and gave herself over to the beat.

"OK. Great energy. Let's go!" Ms. Bennet turned to face the mirror.

Before she could move to her box of music, Maeve called out her own suggestion.

"OK." Ms. Bennet smiled. "Southern hip hop it is. And, Maeve, since you suggested this piece, why don't you and

Tim give us a demonstration to start off the class?"

She couldn't say no. She didn't want to say no. The truth was, she was thrilled. She loved to perform.

Tim reached for her hand, led her into the center of the room, then, just for fun, bowed clear to the floor. But as soon as the music started, the competition was on. The two of them moved in tandem. Maeve was able to follow Tim's lead out of the corner of her eye. She had been watching him for weeks and had been practicing a lot of his moves in the mirror at home. Ready to give it her all, Maeve danced until the sweat was pouring down her face and her heart was pounding a zillion beats per minute.

When the duo had finished, everyone cheered, including Ms. Bennet. "Music video auditions, here they come," she acknowledged proudly. "OK," she motioned to the rest of the class. "Everybody up." The teacher stood at the front of the class, executed a five-step combo, then encouraged the class to repeat it with her.

When Maeve caught her breath, she joined in with the rest of her class, and the remaining forty minutes whizzed by.

She didn't speak to Tim again until class was over, and she was getting her jacket and purse.

"Great moves, Maeve. Hope she teams us up again."

"I do, too, Tim. I thought we looked really together out there." Then she took a deep breath and stuck her neck out. "Do you think I could audition for a video with you?"

Tim didn't answer her, but he did smile.

Back to the Real World

The Beacon Street Girls met at Montoya's Bakery before school on Tuesday morning.

"Hello, girls," Mrs. Montoya greeted warmly. "Good to see all of you survived your week of camping. You are braver than me. I don't like bears or bugs, and I like clean sheets."

"It was really fun, Mrs. Montoya," Isabel enthused. "I was like you before I left, but the woods were beautiful, and I loved hiking up the mountain. I felt like I could do anything by the time I got to the top." She gave the older woman a thumbs-up.

Mrs. Montoya gave Isabel a big smile. "What would you all like to eat?" Isabel could see where Nick Montoya got his good looks. Mrs. Montoya was lovely. She had big brown eyes and her smile revealed lovely, straight white teeth. Isabel thought she could have been a model when she was younger.

"You are a rainbow of color today, Isabel. Muy bonita. A feast for the eyes." Isabel was so pleased with the compliment because she had worn a light green T-shirt decorated with her own drawings of flowers. That morning, Katani said it was magnificent, and now Mrs. Montoya was complimenting her as well.

While she chatted, Mrs. Montoya had been gathering a bag of muffins fresh from the oven. She poured five cups of hot chocolate. "If you will take the muffins, Isabel, I'll carry this tray to your table." She turned and greeted Charlotte with a warm smile, and asked how she had enjoyed Lake Rescue.

The girls paid for their food, thanked Mrs. Montoya, and when they were seated, Isabel handed out the muffins. All of them breathed in the heavenly smell of homemade cocoa with real milk and the aroma of warm cinnamon muffins.

"You are blushing, Charlotte!" Katani said when Mrs. Montoya went back to the counter. "I'll bet Nick talked about you when he was sharing his adventures at Lake Rescue with his mom."

"I am not, Katani. It's the heat from the cocoa," Charlotte insisted. When she looked up and saw Katani's smirky smile, she realized her friend was teasing. Charlotte threw a napkin at her. Meanwhile, Maeve licked away the foam spilling over the top of her drink. "So, what are we wearing to the party? It's a Hawaiian theme."

"The invitation didn't say costumes," Isabel pointed out. "I don't know what I'm wearing yet."

"What party?" Avery said with a puzzled look on her face.

A moment of dead silence came over the other four girls. You could have heard a hot chocolate bubble pop.

"Didn't you get ... um ... your invitation from Julie Faber?" Charlotte stammered, looking desperately around the table for help. But the other BSG just stared at Charlotte.

"Julie gave them out at lunch yesterday. Didn't she give you one?" Charlotte continued, wishing that the room would swallow her up. "Maybe she couldn't find you after school." Charlotte felt Avery had to be invited. She just had to be.

"I saw Julie after school yesterday at the basketball tryouts meeting. She didn't mention anything about a party or an invitation." Avery looked around blankly at her friends.

Maeve looked at Charlotte, then Katani and Isabel. "Maybe we could ask Julie ... she might have forgotten about it. Maybe ... Maybe ..."

"Yeah, well, maybe I'm not invited," Avery said. "Whatever. I'm really busy anyway. Plus, you know me; I'm not really the 'party girl' type." Avery chugged her cocoa and stood up. "I've got to go check my math homework over and hand in my revised book report to Ms. Rodriguez before school starts."

✿

The other girls fell silent as Avery gathered her things. No one knew what to say. Avery gave a tiny wave as she left the table.

Isabel's heart went out to Avery. "What are we going to do?"

"We're not going to the party," Katani announced. "That's an easy decision."

"Right," agreed Isabel, Charlotte, and Maeve.

"I didn't want to go that bad anyway," Katani huffed, putting her nose in the air. "Julie Faber is a snob not to have invited Avery. Besides, remember our rule: Beacon Street Girls forever!"

The BSG clicked their hot chocolate mugs in solidarity. The sound seemed loud in the silence that had surrounded them. Each took a big sip of the sweet liquid and studied their cups.

"Do we really have to skip it?" Maeve asked in a meek voice. "It's going to be the party of the year. You know how Julie's parents always go all out. Hey, they're probably bringing in sand from Hawaii to make a huge beach in the rec room."

"Maeve!" all the BSG shouted.

"You know the BSG have to stick together," Charlotte scolded Maeve, but her expression softened when she saw the disappointment on Maeve's face. Her romantic friend just loved parties. For some reason, in that moment, Charlotte realized that it wasn't just about the fun. Friendly and energetic Maeve could shine at a party where she couldn't shine in school.

"I know, I know." Maeve hung her head. "But given last year's extravaganza it's going to be such a great party."

"They'll probably fly in real orchid leis for all the girls," Katani said wistfully. "You know, like that crazy TV show about the sweet sixteen parties."

"I wasn't here for last year's party," Charlotte reminded them. "Would they really do something like that?"

"They would. Last year Mrs. Faber took about twenty girls to Boston to shop. She gave each of us some money to spend. Afterward, we went to that fancy French restaurant for lunch. I didn't like the food that much, but the shopping was really fun," Katani said, remembering the pretty pair of earrings she had purchased.

"Maybe we could talk Julie into inviting Avery," suggested Maeve, a twinge of hope in her voice.

"Julie could still have Avery's invitation," Charlotte said. "Maybe she just forgot to give it to Avery."

"You really believe that?" Katani asked.

No one answered. They sat quietly for another minute, fearing the truth.

"We have to be loyal to Avery," Charlotte said. "She'd stick up for any of us."

"You are so right about that." Katani finished off her muffin and stood up. "But I lied. I do want to go to Julie's party as much as all of you want to go. But I won't go unless she includes Avery. And even if she invites Avery after we put pressure on her, she's already hurt her feelings. Did you see Avery's face when she left? She was really upset, even if she pretended she wasn't."

"Oh, wow." Isabel looked at her watch. "It's getting late. We have to get to school." The Beacon Street Girls packed up their things and hurried out of the bakery. They were going to be really late if they didn't run. Nobody wanted to get after-school detention.

✿

Who's Invited?

Tuesday morning lasted forever. Maeve survived math by copying equations out of her textbook onto index cards. The Crow had actually complimented her and suggested the rest of the class follow her lead. Under her breath Joline whispered that Maeve probably didn't understand what the equations meant. Maeve made a face at Joline, but at the same time felt horrible inside because she knew Joline was right. The equations looked like gobbledygook to her. Math felt like a giant pit of mud. Could she survive without it? That was the question she had asked Matt, her tutor. He told her that you had to understand math or you could end up in serious trouble with taxes and stuff like that.

At lunch, the BSG were quiet. Avery was missing again. Was this on purpose, or was she studying? They'd also found out that there was a whole "not invited" group: Riley Lee, Betsy Fitzgerald, Chelsea Briggs, and Robert Worley.

Of course, Julie couldn't invite the entire seventh grade, but the fact that she invited only part of a group that were obviously friends and left others out felt really mean to the BSG. It was like inviting Joline Kaminsky and not Anna McMasters. Katani wondered if Julie had excluded Avery on purpose ... just to divide up the BSG.

Of course, Henry Yurt was invited. Julie wouldn't dare leave the class president out. Actually, Henry was becoming quite popular, proving that a zebra can change his stripes. The Yurtmeister was a big joke when he ran for class president, but when he won, people took another look at him. And then to the surprise of everyone, Henry Yurt, father of Pajama Day, started acting like a leader instead of a clown. Except, of course, in math, where Henry had taken it upon himself to liven things up and improve the Crow's sense of humor.

"But, Mrs. Fields," Henry had protested when the Crow had sent him to the principal. "Mr. Sherman is in need of some lightness of spirit. His facial expressions alone can cause a massive attack of negativity."

Katani overheard her grandmother telling her mom the story, and Mrs. Fields said that she had to bite her cheeks to keep from laughing. Katani wished that she could tell the story to her friends, but it was a rule that she couldn't repeat anything Mrs. Fields said at home to people at school. "It would compromise my integrity at school, dear," her grandmother had explained.

"Henry Yurt is going, but not Avery. I just think that is impossibly unfair. But we're not going to solve this problem by sitting around moping," Katani said in her serious executive voice. "Something has to be done!"

"Do you know what to do, besides what we've already decided?" Isabel asked.

"No, but we have to figure something out. This isn't a school problem." Maybe she'd talk to her older sister, who was in college. Candice was a really good advice giver.

"We don't have long to decide," Maeve said. "I have to plan what to wear. Oops!" Maeve knew the minute she'd mentioned clothes, it wasn't the right thing to say. Sure enough, she got the "how insensitive are you?" look from her friends. "I'm sorry. I know clothes aren't important right now. I just can't help myself. It's just where my mind goes."

"Can we talk tonight?" Charlotte stood up. "I'm not very hungry. I guess I'll go over to the newspaper office and work."

The girls agreed, returned their trays, and split up for the rest of the lunch break. Riley Lee caught up with Maeve on the way out of the cafeteria. Soon they were deep in conversation about a music video that Riley had seen.

✿

Sam The Man

Maeve's afternoon got so busy that she almost forgot about the party and the "not invited" list. Right after school she went to math tutoring. Poor Matt, she had whined the whole time. When she arrived home for dinner her mother was rushing about.

"I hope you don't mind Chinese takeout." Ms. Kaplan placed several white containers on the table. "I have a class."

"Wait, Mom, I have Hebrew School, remember?" Maeve usually looked after her younger brother Sam after school and at night if her parents were busy. But since her mother and father separated, her mom seemed to have something extra every night. She seemed to be completely ignoring Maeve's schedule.

"Sam, can you go over to Gary's house until Maeve gets back?" Ms. Kaplan picked up the phone. "It won't be late."

"Yeah!" Sam looked at Maeve and raised his eyebrows clear to his bangs. His friend Gary was a blast and a half.

Ms. Kaplan arranged the visit, promised to let Gary visit Sam another day, and dashed out the door. Sam followed, still chewing.

Hebrew School was in walking distance from the theater. The class was so boring she almost fell asleep. Sometimes Hebrew was as complicated as math to Maeve, but she liked all the stories. Tonight she couldn't wait to get home and look through her closet for something to wear to Julie Faber's party. Her Bat Mitzvah portion would just have to wait.

She arrived home at the same time Gary's mother dropped Sam at the door. No one kept two 8 year-old boys longer than was absolutely necessary.

"I'm still hungry," Sam said. "Gary's mom didn't have any good snacks. She wanted me to eat fruit cocktail. Yuck!"

Maeve gestured to the takeout containers that were still on the kitchen table, half eaten.

"I'm having seconds. Want some?" Sam asked.

"OK. Where's Mom?" Maeve was really hungry, but suddenly the idea of cold Chinese made her feel queasy. She looked in the freezer and pulled out some strawberry ice cream instead. She sliced a banana into what was left in the container and smushed it all together.

"I don't know. You think she has a date?" Sam tried to use chopsticks to pick up a grain of rice.

"I have no idea what Mom is up to. I almost liked it better when she fussed at me all the time."

Maeve had hated all the scheduling and her mother's obsessive attention to "everything Maeve" before her mother and father split up. But now, Maeve was practically feeling neglected. First, the upcoming test she knew she wasn't ready for. Then a party she wasn't going to be able to go to, all because Julie Faber felt like being mean. Maeve had seen a picture of a guy who was trying to carry the world up a mountain on his shoulders. That's how she felt right now. Maeve the Magnificent carrying a pink globe on her shoulders. NO ONE was home to help her.

"What's wrong, Maeve?" Sam asked. "Are you getting ready to cry?"

"I hate math!" Maeve nearly choked on a banana bite.

Finally Sam said, "You'll make the ice cream salty if you cry."

That did it. Now Maeve giggled and stuffed her mouth with sweet, cold spoonfuls of strawberry ice cream. Strawberry was her favorite. Who could not love strawberry ice cream? It was so pink, she thought with pleasure.

"You goin' to Julie's party?" Sam asked.

✿

"How do you know about that?" Maeve asked back.

"Gary's sister is going and he says she's making him sick with all the planning about what to wear." Sam attacked the grains of rice again.

"NO! I'm not going!" Maeve was practically yelling. She tried to calm down. She took a deep breath. "Julie didn't invite Avery, who is practically my best friend in the whole world, along with Charlotte, Katani, and Isabel. So none of us are going. So, we're going to do something with Avery instead. We're making a statement!"

The class had just talked about people making a statement in social studies. Rosa Parks had died. She was noted in history as the black woman who refused to give up her seat on the bus to a white man. She figured she paid her fare. She deserved the seat as much as anyone. She had no idea that her actions were going to spark an entire movement in the South. Now, that was really making a statement. But ordinary people could make a statement over little things, too. Not that Julie's snub was equal to what happened to Rosa Parks, but it was excluding someone she knew, thought Maeve.

Maeve came out of her daydream to see that Sam was frowning. He appeared to be thinking about what making a statement meant.

"It means—"

"I know what it means. It's like when Mom buys me clothes that nobody, I mean nobody, is wearing, and I wear my old torn jeans and stained Blue Guys T-shirt."

Maeve closed her eyes and sighed. "Do you think Mom is losing it, Sam?"

"I guess. But there's nothing we can do about it."

Sam tried to grab some food and missed. He gave up on his chopsticks, speared a chunk of sesame chicken with his knife, and poked it in his mouth. "I could help you with your math. I already know fractions!"

"Sam, if you tutored me, we would get in the biggest fight of our lives. And even though I'm having trouble, I'm so beyond third-grade math. But thanks for offering anyway."

"What are you going to do about Julie and the Hawaiian party?" he asked, slurping up a noodle.

Maeve couldn't believe it. She was actually sitting at the kitchen table having a real conversation with Sam. Was this real, or was she so desperate for conversation that she would sit and chat with anyone, even her little brother?

"No. Well, yes, not go. We've all decided we won't go without Avery."

"But you love parties, don't you?" Sam took the other side of the argument in Maeve's head.

"Yeah, Sam. I love parties. I am *really* good at parties."

Maeve could see herself dancing with Dillon. Then all of a sudden Riley popped into her head. Maeve and Riley could talk about music for hours. Like this afternoon. It was so much fun having a heated discussion with Riley about his fave new band. And they were planning another song for her to sing with his band. She could dance with Riley and Dillon. She would be wearing the orchid lei. Eating coconuts and pineapples. Both boys would bring her punch in a cup made from a coconut shell that had a little umbrella. She'd take a deep breath of the sweet perfume of Hawaii. Reality check. Riley wasn't invited to the party. That was so mean, thought Maeve.

"What should we do about all this food?" asked Sam.

"I don't know. Put it away. Eat it. Don't eat all of it, though. You'll be sick."

"I know that. I'm not a—"

✿

"I know. You really aren't a baby, Sam." Maeve turned around and hugged her brother.

"Ugh. Get away from me." Sam pretended he was going to sword fight Maeve with his chopsticks, but he was smiling.

Maeve smiled back, helped Sam clean up the kitchen, and hurried off to bed before the good feelings about Sam faded.

Just as she was falling asleep, she felt her mother kiss her lightly on the cheek. "Thank you, sweetheart, for taking care of Sam and cleaning up the kitchen. You are my special girl."

Maeve murmured, "I love you," to her mom.

CHAPTER 3

FAIR PLAY

CHARLOTTE HEARD Avery call from downstairs, "Char, it's me." She was a little surprised to hear her friend's voice.

Usually Avery called the night before when she was coming over early to walk Marty. She ran halfway up the elegant staircase, then slid down the banister while Charlotte and Marty ran after her.

"What are you doing here, Ave?" Charlotte asked.

"Just felt like it. And I missed Marty. You missed me, too, didn't you, little guy?" Avery grabbed Marty up in her arms and the little dog licked her face.

Just as Charlotte, Avery, and Marty were heading out the door, Miss Pierce suddenly appeared.

"Charlotte, why don't you stop by for tea and cookies some afternoon?" she called after them. "I have some wonderful new images from the Hubble telescope. I think you would find them fascinating, and my new recipe for Chocolate Coconut Surprises is scrumptious."

"Wow, I'd love to, Miss Pierce," Charlotte said. "But right now, Marty is going to have a heart attack if we don't walk him." The little dog was practically hopping on one leg.

"I see that. Run along, girls, run along." Miss Pierce patted Charlotte on the shoulder as the girls rushed outside. Charlotte was so surprised. Usually Miss Pierce refrained from any physical contact. She was so shy.

"Maybe she is starting to come out of her shell," Charlotte said to Avery when they got outside. "How nice of her to invite me. I'd love to see some Hubble photos."

Charlotte's landlord was a mysterious recluse, but Miss Pierce had so many hobbies she kept busy night and day. She was an astronomer who studied deep space. Before they knew anything about Miss Pierce, the BSG had discovered her telescope up in the Tower. She worked for NASA and was always getting packages and visits from men in black. Charlotte wondered what secret assignments they might be giving Miss Pierce. Avery was convinced that Miss Pierce was researching aliens. Isabel said she didn't want to think of alien visitations—little green men with black holes for eyes gave her the willies.

"I think Marty missed us when we went to Lake Rescue." Charlotte pulled on her vintage denim jacket—the one that had belonged to her mother years ago. It was the most important piece of clothing Charlotte owned, and she hoped it would last forever.

Marty jumped and barked and wagged his stub of a tail as if to say, yes, I missed you BSG, and now you need to make up for leaving me practically alone. But meanwhile, wanna see me dance? See how high I can jump?

"I know he missed us. Huh, boy!" Avery bounced beside the little dog.

The outside air was autumn brisk with a hint of rain. Charlotte savored all the seasons and loved having them change. But, Charlotte didn't want any more change. She'd had all she could handle for a long time. She and her father had moved so often after Charlotte's mother died. Now Charlotte felt she could live in Brookline and in the old Victorian house forever.

"Let's jog. Marty needs the exercise." Avery picked up the pace.

Charlotte didn't feel like running. "Can we just walk fast?"

"OK." Avery bent down to pat Marty on his funny little head.

"Avery," Charlotte took a deep breath and jumped in. "We decided that none of us are going to Julie Faber's party. If you aren't invited, we aren't going. That's totally unfair for Julie to leave you out. She knows that all of us are best friends."

"Well, I'm not best friends with Julie. I don't even like Julie Fabulous Faber." Avery looked away as she spoke. "And I don't want you to stay home because of me. Then I'll feel like a total loser. *Avery wasn't invited, and we're going to stay home and make her feel good*. No, I want all of you to go."

"But, Ave. We want …"

Avery stopped to pick up Marty's little chew toy Happy Lucky Thingy. She threw it and the perky little dog flew off after it. He was back in seconds for another throw.

"Forget it, Charlotte. I don't want to talk about this."

Charlotte gulped. She didn't want Avery to be uncomfortable. She just wanted her friend to know that the BSG were loyal. Everybody they knew was going to the party. What would Avery do that night?

When they caught up to Marty the second time, he was shaking his toy as hard as he could. Happy Lucky Thingy was the only thing Avery had brought with her from Korea when she was adopted as a baby. It was a testament to how much she adored Marty that she would give him the toy. Avery growled and stood tall, her hands over her head, then brought them down, pretending to attack Marty.

Marty was ecstatic. He'd play with his girl Avery all day.

Charlotte took a deep breath and stopped to look at a flower bed. "Don't you love zinnias?"

Avery smiled in spite of her sad feelings about the party. Charlotte could be so quirky sometimes.

"How's your ankle?" Charlotte asked.

"Not too bad. I'm so glad that I didn't break it or sprain it worse. I felt so stupid getting hurt anyway." Avery was relieved to be talking about ankles and sports instead of parties.

They walked slowly back to Charlotte's, talking about basketball and newspaper work and avoiding the one topic Charlotte wanted to talk about. Charlotte glanced at her watch. They were OK on time. Before she could say anything more to Avery, her friend turned to her.

"Charlotte, you have to promise me that you, Isabel, Katani, and Maeve will go to the Fabulous Faber's party. Especially Maeve. I know she wants to go really bad. Maeve just loves parties. Dillon was invited, and I'm sure Nick was, too. You want to go. You know you do. So … please, just go."

"But—"

"Someone needs to stay home and dog-sit. Right, Marty?"

"Ruffff," Marty agreed. "Ruff."

"Promise, you'll all go, Charlotte?" Avery looked at her friend.

Charlotte sighed but she nodded yes.

They tucked Marty inside the house, grabbed their book bags, which they had left inside the front door, and took off down Corey Hill. Charlotte waved to Yuri, who was just about the first friend she had made in Brookline. Charlotte noticed that today Yuri had bouquets of fall flowers, all the varieties and colors she'd seen in the park. They coordinated with the fall vegetables. Sometimes she wished she could paint. She needed to think about how to write a poem about colors changing with the seasons. *Colors wild and true* ... that could be the first line, she thought.

They skipped past Party Favors—and according to Avery, home of the best chocolate cupcakes in the world—then turned left onto Harvard Street. Crowds of kids mingled outside Abigail Adams Junior High, all of them glad the rain had stopped and the sky was clear.

Every group of seventh graders they passed, it seemed, was talking about Julie's party. What they were going to wear, what things Julie might have planned. Charlotte and Avery pretended they didn't hear the buzz, although Charlotte noticed that Avery's cheeks were flushed. They ran up the steps, slipped into the busy hall, and hurried to their lockers. Charlotte felt sorry for her friend, and she wondered if Julie Faber knew how it felt to be left out.

Maeve was the first to see them. "Hi, guys. What's up?"

"Charlotte and I took Marty for a walk," Avery said. "He was tired of being cooped up. He needed to conduct a squirrel raid."

"I can't believe you can get up so early. I have to be dragged out of bed." Maeve yawned. "I'll walk Marty after school on Friday if I'm not grounded forever."

"Are you still obsessing over that math test?" Avery tossed books into her locker and pulled out a couple. "It's no big deal."

"Maybe not to you, but what if I fail? It could be the end of the world as I know it." Maeve's face was so long, they bit their lips to keep from laughing.

"I can help you study, Maeve," Katani said.

Katani never got nervous on tests and was so organized, she had probably been prepared days ago.

Maeve tried to make a joke of the whole thing, but Charlotte could see the panic oozing out of her friend's pores. And today was only Wednesday.

"You have two days left to study," Isabel said.

"My tutor almost gave up on me last night. I don't think anyone can help me. I am doomed."

Going Out for the Team

That afternoon, Avery and Isabel headed to the gym for basketball tryouts. Avery was excited, but she still couldn't stop thinking about not being invited to Julie Faber's party. Avery wasn't used to not getting picked. She was always one of the first people chosen for sports teams and even for academic groups at school, because she was also a good student. She wasn't friends with Julie, but neither were Charlotte or Isabel, so why was Avery the only one left out?

Avery glanced at Isabel as they arrived at the gym doors. Maybe she could talk to Isabel about being left out of the party. But Isabel was invited, so Avery didn't want to make her feel bad by complaining about it. Avery had almost talked to her brother Scott that morning before school. Normally he was a good listener and gave good advice, but Avery didn't think Scott would understand—he was always invited to everything.

This party thing was just too confusing. She took a deep breath as she walked across the gym floor to the bleachers. Avery tried to stop thinking about parties and to start thinking about a much more pleasant topic: basketball.

"Isn't this great, Isabel!"

"Yeah, I guess ... But I'm so nervous!" said Isabel as she adjusted her knee brace. Isabel had injured her knee ballet dancing and had to wear a protective brace. "Maybe I shouldn't have let you talk me into trying out. What if I make a fool of myself?"

"Don't worry, Izzy," Avery said reassuringly. "You'll do awesome! Being confident is half the battle."

"But I've never played on a real team before, just at the park in my old neighborhood."

"Think positive, Isabel. You know all the rules and you already know how to shoot ... so you're all set!"

"Thanks Avery, you know, I think you're right!" Isabel was starting to feel less nervous after Avery's pep talk. "Hey, is that Betsy Fitzgerald?"

Avery looked toward the gym door and was surprised to see Betsy Fitzgerald, teacher's pet and class know-it-all, walking into the gym dressed for tryouts. "I didn't know Betsy played basketball."

"And there's Anna and Julie Faber," said Isabel, looking around to scope out the competition. There was a group of eighth graders standing together at the end of the bleachers. "Those eighth graders are so tall!"

"Well, being tall isn't everything," commented Avery with a smile. Avery was the shortest girl in their class, but she made up for it by being really quick on the court and always playing hard.

Coach Porter called all the girls over to the bleachers to explain how tryouts would work. They would have two days of competition. The first day, they would be working on some simple dribbling, passing, and shooting drills. The second day would concentrate on defense and game play.

"I'm pleased to see such a great turnout. I'm really excited about this season, and I hope you're all ready to work hard and most importantly, have a lot of fun! We'll start off with warmups, then we'll get into the drills." Coach Porter was really enthusiastic. "OK girls, let's get started!"

For the first half hour, the girls ran through dribbling and passing drills. Avery knew most of the girls that were trying out from the many teams she had played on since elementary school. Everybody was working hard to impress the coach with their basketball skills.

Avery thought that Isabel was doing great, and she really hoped she would make the team. It would be so fun to have another BSG on the basketball team. She was really surprised to see that Betsy Fitzgerald actually knew how to play. Avery had always thought that Betsy was only interested in getting into college.

Julie Faber was also a pretty good player, which really annoyed Avery. She had been hoping that Julie wouldn't make the team, and then maybe Julie could be the one who was left out. But if she did make the team ... well, Avery would deal with that when it happened. For now, she had to concentrate on making the team herself.

Coach Porter blew her whistle. "Now we're moving on to shooting drills. First, I'd like to see everyone practice free throws. We'll split into two groups, one at each basket. Let's count off 1-2-1-2, and the 1s will be at the other basket and the 2s will stay here."

The girls counted off 1-2-1-2. Avery was a 2, and so were Isabel, Betsy, Julie, and a bunch of eighth graders, including Amanda Cruz, who had been the star of the team last year.

"OK, everyone get in line at the top of the key. You'll all take ten free throws each turn. Free throws are a very important part of the game, and everyone can improve their percentage with practice."

Avery and the other girls jogged over to form a line. Avery was third in line, right behind Betsy. Amanda Cruz was up first, and she got seven out of ten.

"Great job, Amanda," said Coach Porter, as she made some marks on her clipboard. "Alright Betsy, you're up next."

Avery heard someone giggling behind her. She looked over her shoulder and realized it was Julie Faber and a tall eighth grader, Sarah Meyers, who appeared to be laughing at Betsy.

"Did you see her sneakers?" Julie whispered to Sarah.

"Those are so fifth grade," Sarah sneered. "I can't believe she thinks she would actually make the team. As if."

Avery couldn't believe how snobby Julie and Sarah were being. Who cared if Betsy's sneakers were "last year." Fashion didn't matter in basketball!

Betsy was calmly bouncing the basketball at the line as she prepared to start taking free throws, acting like she couldn't hear Julie and Sarah. She carefully lined up her shot, bent her knees, and sent the ball sailing in a perfect arc, straight into the hoop.

"Go Betsy!" Avery whooped and everybody but Julie and Sarah clapped.

Betsy smiled and continued to make her foul shots, one after another until she had made nine in a row. She was shooting better than Amanda, who was the star of the team. Everyone was shocked. Betsy took her tenth shot and it swished right through the net. Who knew?

"Awesome job, Betsy. Ten for ten!" Coach Porter was excited to see such a great shooter. "Let's see if anyone can match that!"

Everyone else took their turn, but no one managed to

match Betsy's record. Avery was pretty happy with getting seven out of ten, and Isabel got six out of ten. They finished up tryouts that day with practicing lay-ups, and Avery noticed that Betsy missed every one she attempted. How could she be so good at free throws but so bad at lay-ups?

"Hey Betsy," Avery said as she headed to the locker room after tryouts, "great job on those free throws!"

"Thanks. I've been practicing. Practice makes perfect, you know. Every night, after I finish my homework, I've been shooting fifty free throws. My cousin Colleen got a full athletic scholarship to Princeton. My dream is to go there, too, and I thought maybe basketball could be my ticket in." Betsy was kind of crazy, but her hard work did seem to pay off.

"Wow, that's cool." Avery admired anyone who worked hard, tried their best, and sometimes surprised themselves. But, sometimes, Betsy was over the top with her college obsession.

Overall, Avery thought that tryouts had gone really well. Isabel had played great, and Betsy was the surprise star of foul shots. Maybe a lot of seventh graders would make the team. If only Julie Faber wasn't trying out, then Avery could really forget about her party.

CHAPTER 4

SO NOT FAIR

"I JUST DON'T GET THIS, Matt, I don't." Maeve was ready to throw her math book across the room. "I'm math impaired. Admit it and give up on me. Algebra, geometry, all these fractions, equations, and word problems. I hate word problems. They're so frustrating. Who cares about two trains traveling at different speeds and what time they arrive someplace? I'll just call a travel agent when I want to travel and say, 'Get me the best schedule.'"

Good-natured Matt had been Maeve's math tutor for some time now, and he was used to seeing her get frustrated. He was also used to her being melodramatic. Her flair for the dramatic made Maeve one of his favorite students. And he was a good tutor, really patient. Maeve knew she shouldn't push him too far though—she didn't want to have to get used to someone else and have to explain all over again how math made no sense to her.

Matt made a suggestion to Maeve. "Try to relax, Maeve, maybe you're trying too hard and that's making you block out everything. Research has shown—"

"Matt," Maeve groaned. "I don't care what research says. What does research know about Maeve Kaplan-Taylor? Nothing. No one ever came to me and said, 'We want to research why you can't learn math.' I'm not in their silly studies. And don't keep telling me, 'If you relax it will come.' That's like that line in that baseball movie, 'If you build it, they will come.' So I relax, and I still don't get it. You think a bunch of math geniuses will sit there beside me during the test and feed me answers? I don't think so."

The verbal avalanche left Maeve exhausted. She flopped back onto the chair at the kitchen table and covered her face with both hands.

"Maeve, you've panicked over this particular test. If you just try to take a few deep breaths, take each problem slowly, and do your best, I know you can pass."

"That's easy for you to say, Matt. You've already passed seventh-grade math and eighth and senior high and you're in college. What if I never make it out of seventh grade? I'll be stuck at Abigail Adams Junior High forever, and you'll still be tutoring me when you're 80 years old!"

"I'll have a beard and I'll hand you cheat sheets from under it. In the meantime ... breathe."

"I'm too desperate to breathe." Maeve grabbed a carrot stick and crunched it as if she were attacking a math theorem. Why hadn't her mother bought snacks with more substance? She wanted a brownie or chocolate chip cookies. You need chocolate for math, Maeve reasoned. Suddenly, she jumped up to look in the cupboard. She thought she remembered some M&Ms.

Matt took a deep breath and turned the page to more problems. "Let's try a few more, Maeve. Practicing does make it easier."

I think I'm going to need a calculator ...
EGGONOMICS
Isabel M.

✿

The numbers blurred when Maeve tried to look at them. The page might as well have been written in Chinese.

One time a teacher showed her mother and father a page of Chinese and asked them to read it. She had made her point. "When kids first learn to read, the page looks like this to them. For Maeve, some of the words still look like Chinese," the teacher explained. "Somehow, we're still trying to understand how her brain reverses some of the letters for her. So she has to decode twice. Reverse the words back, then read the word. She has to do twice the work that most kids have to when they learn to read. It's an extremely frustrating experience." Maeve remembered thinking, *now they will fix me.*

Well, now Maeve felt as if she was doing twice or maybe four times the work other kids do when they learn math.

"It's not fair," Maeve said in a quiet voice.

"Most of life isn't fair, Maeve. Why can you dance and sing like a Broadway star while I croak like a frog and look like I need medication on the dance floor?" Matt laughed at his own joke.

"I guess I'll have to get through life on my talent since I have this upside down, reversible brain," Maeve replied.

"Yeah, maybe you could do that, but you still need math so nobody steals your money. Let's try one more time."

Matt grinned, and Maeve felt as if she'd try ten more times for him.

They worked a little longer, taking one problem at a time. Often, when Matt read the problem out loud to her, she caught on faster. Maybe her math problem was a reading problem.

"What is this problem asking?" Matt said when they'd both read it aloud.

"It's asking how much money I'd have left. Probably none, since I'd spend the remainder on a new blouse."

"OK, how much would you have to spend on a new blouse?"

When Matt asked something practical like that, something Maeve really wanted to know, she could figure it out.

"You like money, Maeve?" Matt asked.

"Yeah?" Maeve said, looking suspiciously at Matt.

"We can pretend all these numbers are money. Would that help you figure them out?"

"Maybe." She tried to do as Matt said, and they did make more than usual progress that day. But Maeve still felt discouraged. Matt would not be sitting next to her at the test.

After Matt left, she sat at the table, exhausted. Finally she put her head down on her math book and actually fell asleep.

"Do you think the math will soak into your brain while you sleep, honey?" her mother said, waking Maeve by touching her on the shoulder.

Maeve came back to the real world, to the table cluttered with scribbled numbers. "I'm going to fail, Mom. Even with Matt's help. I can't possibly pass the math test on Friday. I'm just stupid, really stupid." Maeve broke down, crying as if her heart was broken. What a waste, a broken heart over math instead of Dillon or someone equally cute.

She didn't know how long she sat there, tears running down her face, thinking about Dillon and Riley and music and parties and dancing. All of her friends were good at math. Charlotte and Katani were practically geniuses, and Isabel and Avery got Bs and sometimes Cs. If Maeve got a C on a big math test, her family would have a celebration. The problem was she got Ds and sometimes Fs. Nobody would ever celebrate for her.

Maeve didn't even hear her mother make the phone call, but knew she must have done so when a few minutes later

✿

her father sat beside her and took her arm.

"Maeve, Sweetheart, you have to calm down. One test is not the end of the world."

By then, Maeve didn't have much crying left inside. She didn't have much of anything left inside. In fact, she realized she was hungry. How could she be hungry when life as she knew it was coming to an abrupt end?

"I—I—maybe I'm just hungry."

Mr. Taylor hugged Maeve and gave his wife a tender smile. Maeve caught it out of the corner of her eye. A flutter of hope came over her. But it passed so quickly Maeve thought maybe it was just her stomach growling.

Her father stood up, glad he'd found something he really could do to help. "Well, that's easily fixed. Let's go get something wonderful to eat. Do you mind if Sam goes? Then your mother doesn't have to prepare dinner."

"Why doesn't Mom come with us?" Maeve looked at her mother, who smiled but shook her head.

"I have homework, too. I can eat a microwave dinner and work right here in the math wreckage."

"It could rub off on you," Maeve warned. "You might never understand your contracts or whatever it is you brought home."

"I'll take that chance." Her mother hugged her, wiped her eyes, and said, "Run upstairs and wash your face. Put on a clean shirt. You'll feel better."

Recovering from the major meltdown was going to take longer than Dad would wait. Quickly Maeve washed her face and got ready to go. She pinched her cheeks for some color and threw a lip gloss into her pocket. You never knew who you might run into eating out. Math was suddenly not so important.

"That's better," her dad said when she got back to the kitchen. He put his arm around her and steered her toward the door.

Sam bounced, kicked, and punched the air as they headed for the car. "Can we have pizza?"

"Tonight is Maeve's choice, Sam. You choose next time."

"That's not fair. It's my turn." He crouched into a kung fu position and leaped into a fight stance.

"Does he have to come?" she implored her father. The idea of walking into a restaurant with a Mutant Ninja Turtle was not her idea of a relaxing dinner.

"Sam," her father spoke sharply. "Behave yourself. We are taking your sister out to cheer her up."

Looking at the defeated face of her brother, Maeve said, "I guess pizza sounds good."

In the car, Maeve stared out the window. Life wasn't only not fair, it was strange and more often than not, totally confusing. She had been so upset about math a minute ago, and now she was listening to Sam blather on about Tae Kwon Do class to her dad. Maybe she would be OK for the test.

Sisters

Isabel's life wasn't running smoothly either.

"You promised, Izzy. You promised me a long time ago!"

Elena Maria, Isabel's older sister, stomped her foot and paced around the kitchen. Her dark eyes flashed fire. Usually the way Isabel handled Elena's hot temper was to leave. But she couldn't. This involved her. And besides, she had to help set the table.

"You can't back out now. I told the Fergusons I'd babysit. When I had a conflict and you promised me you'd fill in. My reputation is on the line here." Elena Maria banged a plate down on the kitchen table as if to emphasize her point.

Isabel didn't remember ever promising that she'd baby-sit. Normally, she wouldn't mind filling in, but the job happened to be the same night as Julie Faber's party.

"I'm sorry, Elena, but I'm going to a party that night. It's going to be 'the party of the year.' I have to be there. Why don't you ask one of your friends to baby-sit?" Isabel felt bad for Elena Maria, but she was starting to get annoyed at her sister's whining.

"All my friends have plans that night. I've already called around. So you have to keep your promise. Isabel, this is really important to me."

"You promised the Fergusons in the first place, so I think you're the one who has to keep your promise, Elena." Isabel was getting a little confused with all of the promises. All she knew was that she *had* to go to the party.

"Come on, Isabel, it's only a seventh-grade birthday party," Elena Maria said. "Listen, I'll do the dishes for two weeks if you just baby-sit for me. It's not even a hard job. They only have two kids."

"Yeah," Isabel raised her voice. "The Fergusons—escapees from the zoo."

"They're not that bad, Izzy. Maybe you could get one of your friends to go with you. It'll be fun!" Elena Maria had a way of sugar-coating her words until Isabel said yes, but Isabel wasn't caving this time.

"If it's going to be so fun, then why don't you baby-sit?" Isabel knew that would set Elena off again, but she'd had enough. She *hated* baby-sitting the Ferguson twins. Everyone did. They were so spoiled. Just because they had starred in a famous commercial about eating cereal and had their own fan club, they thought they were TV stars. And TV stars can do anything they like according to Jamie Ferguson. Stay up all night, eat too much candy or soda, no problem. Talk back when they please, and run through the house like a pair of hyenas on too much caffeine—par for the course. The Fergusons should come with a warning label: *Don't baby-sit these kids!* Isabel got a headache just thinking about baby-sitting them again.

Mrs. Martinez came into the kitchen and the girls stopped their bickering instantly. They continued to set the table in silence. No one wanted to upset Mrs. Martinez.

"Isabel, my dear little sister, could you please get the silverware?" Elena Maria's voice dripped with honey.

Isabel wanted to throw the napkins she was carrying in her dear older sister's face. Instead, she made a face, which made her feel better for the moment.

"What is all this fighting? I could hear you yelling all over the house. You should respect each other, girls. How many times have I told you that?"

"Sorry, Mama," Isabel said. Isabel felt bad that their silly argument had upset their mom. Ever since their mother had gotten sick, the girls tried not to argue. Isabel was glad to see her mother using her walker rather than her wheelchair. That meant she was feeling stronger.

"Si, lo siento, Mama." Elena Maria sent Isabel a fierce look that said, "Don't worry Mama about this." As if Elena Maria hadn't been the one to start the fight in the first place.

Aunt Lourdes came into the kitchen to see if the cheese on the casserole was browned. She pronounced it perfect and lifted it out of the oven. "No problema, Esperanza. It is normal for sisters to fight sometimes."

"Did you and Mama ever fight?" Isabel asked.

Aunt Lourdes set the casserole on the table and laughed.

"Oh, yes, we fought, almost every day. Your mama is a feisty one, let me tell you. There was this one time …"

"No, no stories, Lourdes." Mama shook her head. "Don't encourage them. What you're arguing about, girls?"

Isabel shook her head and placed some of the tamale casserole on her plate. The spicy smell of corn, tomatoes, and shredded chicken filled her nose and she took a big bite. Perfect. Aunt Lourdes was such a good cook. Her homemade tamales were almost as good as Mama's chicken empanadas.

"Actually, Isabel and I were discussing a party she wants to go to. It's at Julie Faber's house. I don't think you should let her go, Mama." Elena Maria smiled sweetly at Isabel.

"Aie, wait a minute, Elena, who made you the mother here?" Isabel felt the cayenne pepper in the casserole go straight to her head. "You can't decide what I can or can't do. You just want me to stay home so—"

Mama put out her hand to hush Isabel. "Why do you say that, Elena Maria? I would like to know."

"I've heard some really bad things about Julie's older brother Bobby and his parties. They're totally out of control, and there's alcohol."

Isabel gasped. She couldn't believe that Elena Maria was trying to sabotage her party plans. Elena knew it was only a junior high party and there was no way it would be out of control. She was just trying to scare their mama into saying that Isabel couldn't go, and so that Isabel would have no excuse not to baby-sit. It was totally unfair.

"This is not Julie's brother's party. And Bobby won't even be there. It's Julie's birthday party. Why don't you just stay out of it? It has nothing to do with you."

"I'm just warning you. I've heard that Julie gets her way on everything she wants."

"So I'm supposed to stay home because you've heard some rumors?"

"Girls, girls." Mama pleaded.

Aunt Lourdes jumped up and got Mama water. "You shouldn't get excited, Esperanza. See what you've done, girls. Your mother needs to eat, rest, and not get excited."

Isabel and Elena Maria looked guiltily across the table at each other.

Isabel knew better. Both of them knew better than to make Mama upset. She was having a hard enough time just fighting her MS. She didn't need squabbling daughters to upset her.

"Sorry, Mama." Elena Maria said. "Are you all right? Try to eat. We'll stop fighting."

Isabel shot Elena a look that said, "It's your fault," but she apologized too. "Lo siento, Mama. Let's all enjoy Aunt Lourdes' good tamales. And thank you again, Aunt Lourdes, for inviting us to live here with you. For putting up with Elena and me as well as taking care of Mama."

"It is my privilege to take care of my sister when she needs help," Aunt Lourdes said, "but I need everyone's cooperation. You girls have to love each other and solve your problems quietly. I'm sure that's possible, isn't it?"

"Si." Both Isabel and Elena ducked their heads down and concentrated on eating.

After dinner, while the two of them were washing dishes, Isabel said, "OK, Elena, I'll baby-sit for you."

"Go—I'll finish up the dishes. You can use the computer."

Isabel dried her hands and hurried to her half of the bedroom. She turned on their PC and entered her password.

✿

Chat Room: BSG

File Edit People View Help

lafrida: I have a problem
skywriter: tell all. we're trying 2 decide what to wear to Julie's party
lafrida: I'm wearing sweatpants and a sweatshirt
flikchic: you're kidding!
lafrida: yeah, I'm kidding. I'm not going 2 the party
Kgirl: why not? I was counting on some Hawaiian design skirt you and I create together
lafrida: I'll help you design a skirt, but I have to baby-sit for Elena. She has a date
flikchic: you're baby-sitting instead of going to the party of the year? The BSG are dropping like flies
lafrida: yeah, Elena says I promised her. but guess what I heard from Elena
skywriter: spill it
lafrida: when Julie's brother Bobby has a party, there's been drinking

Chat Room: BSG
File Edit People View Help
flikchic: no way! That's just a rumor
lafrida: just passing on what I heard
flikchic: Julie's mom won't let her have alcohol. we'll probably have coconut halves filled with pineapple juice
Kgirl: the pineapples will be flown in fresh from Hawaii with the orchid leis
skywriter: we'll get dizzy from smelling the orchids
flikchic: or spinning around while we're dancing
lafrida: where's Avery?
skywriter: i don't know
lafrida: hey, Avery thinks I might make the basketball team
flikchic: you went out for basketball?
lafrida: yeah, I like it. And guess who's the best free-throw shooter at Abigail Adams?
skywriter: Avery, of course
lafrida: NO, wrong answer! Betsy Fitzgerald. LOL
4 people here
lafrida
skywriter
flikchic
Kgirl

✿

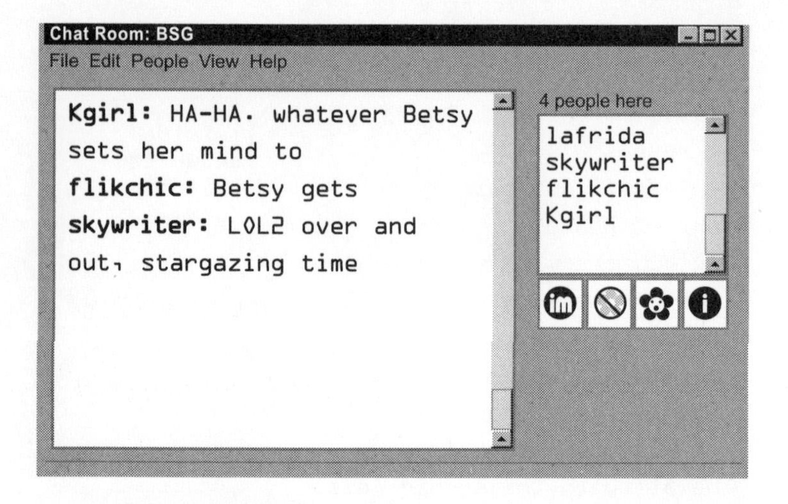

Everyone logged off. Isabel was glad she didn't wait to tell her friends that she wasn't going to the party. It wouldn't have been fair to pull out at the last minute.

Isabel got ready for bed, then ran downstairs to give her mother a big hug. No party mattered as much as Mama. Nothing was as important as her getting better ... and she was getting better. Papa would be so happy when he came to visit. Maybe they could all go to the movies together. Mama loved the movies. She said that she wished she had been an actress. Isabel thought her mother was pretty enough to have been a movie star.

CHAPTER 5

CAN MATH MAKE YOU SICK?

BY THIRD PERIOD on Friday, Maeve had a headache, a queasy stomach, and was sure she was coming down with something really lethal. Maybe malaria, yellow fever, or even bubonic plague.

"How do you get bubonic plague?" she asked Charlotte, who had traveled so much, surely she knew about every disease in the world.

"From rats to fleas. Ancient Europe had such bad sanitary conditions, rats and fleas were everywhere. That's why so many people died. Why are you asking, Maeve? Are you writing a report on world diseases for history?"

"Does Marty have fleas?" Maeve had a one-track mind.

"No. We keep him really clean, and he has a flea collar."

"Then maybe it's yellow fever." With a dramatic sweep of her hand, Maeve took out a tissue and wiped the perspiration from her brow. "Like in that old movie *Yellow Jack*, where Major Walter Reed and all those doctors went to Cuba and let mosquitoes bite them to prove they carried yellow fever. Of course, they all got sick and some of them died as heroes for science and medicine."

Maeve got most of her history from old movies. She just had to hope the stories were accurate. It was a lot more fun learning that way. She especially enjoyed the old black-and-white movies her father picked for the film festivals.

"Yellow fever comes from mosquitoes, but I don't think anyone has had it for a long time. Now West Nile—"

"That's it! I must have West Nile virus. Look, I have a mosquito bite." Maeve pointed to a small red bump on her arm. "How long does it take from the time you get a bite until you're in bed dying?"

"A few days. But not many people die of West Nile, Maeve. Plus, it's too cold for mosquitoes now. This doesn't have anything to do with today's math test, does it?" Charlotte held back a smile but Maeve saw it.

"You can laugh all you want, but I'm sick. I'm really sick. I think I need to go home right now."

"You want me to go to the office with you?" Concerned, Charlotte looked at her watch. "I think we have time, but I'll need to get to math class so I have the full fifty minutes for the test."

If Maeve went to the office now, she'd miss the test, but then she'd have to take it later. Another week of not sleeping. Maeve agonized over her choices, taking the test now and failing, or taking the test next week and failing. At least after this last tutoring session, her dad had called Mr. Sherman and reminded him to let Maeve take her test untimed in the resource room. That might help take the pressure off.

"Do you have any mints? I guess I'd better go take the test and then see how I feel."

"That's probably a good idea." Charlotte searched and handed Maeve a peppermint she found at the bottom of her purse. "It may be a little bit linty, but these are good."

"I don't care if it has mud on it." Maeve grabbed the mint, unwrapped it, and let the minty flavor run through her mouth and slide down her throat. "Thanks, that's good."

The Crow greeted her at the door. Maeve thought she saw a glint of something diabolical in his eyes when he looked at her. When everyone was seated, he walked to the front of the room. In a great show of crow-like excitement, he began to wave a stack of tests about.

"Good morning, class. I know all of you are as *eager* as I am to see just how much math you've learned so far this year. I have great expectations for all of you. If you finish early, I suggest you go back over your test carefully and make sure you've answered every question. Remember, even if you get stumped, show your work. Partial credit is better than none. Any questions?" The Crow was so excited; his eyes looked like two lumps of burning coal. Maeve wished, hoped, really, that he would just start melting like the Wicked Witch of the West. Then, the test would be cancelled. She could go to the cafeteria and socialize with her friends, maybe even get to say hello to Tim. Her dance partner had been very friendly lately, saying hi to her in the halls.

"Ms. Taylor-Kaplan, are you with us?" The Crow was standing over her desk. Was he smirking at her? Maeve's palms began to sweat.

Lisa Chen waved her hand. "But what if we do finish early, check over the test, and feel very satisfied that we've done our best?" Isabel gave Maeve a quick smile. Usually, Maeve loved The Lisa Show. Today, however, she could only manage a wan smile in return.

"Then, by all means, Lisa, find something to read." Mr. Sherman smiled his toothiest smile at Lisa, while his big black unibrow bounced up and down. She was probably his favorite student in the entire world.

Everybody was so stressed about the test that even the class cutups—Dillon, the Yurtmeister, and Billy T.—couldn't manage their favorite imitation of what they called "the Crow Brow Bounce."

Maeve had heard little past the word "eager" and then Lisa asking if they could leave early if they were finished. Peppermint saliva ran down her throat the wrong way and she choked. She coughed uncontrollably until Dillon reached over and pounded her on the back.

"Maeve is so eager," Joline said, only loud enough for those around them to hear.

"Eager to find a way to escape before she even looks at the test." Anna laughed as did everyone around them.

"Maeve will be taking her test in another room," Mr. Sherman said, making a big show of handing her a sealed envelope that felt as if it weighed a thousand pounds. Great, Maeve winced. Not only was she singled out by the Queens of Mean, but now the Crow had just announced that she was the biggest math idiot in the class. Why didn't he just tell everyone that she was "special" and had to take her test somewhere else. So much for just walking quietly out of the room.

"The rest of you, time to get to work." Mr. Sherman cruised the room, watching people. He was getting ready to swoop down on anyone he thought was cheating.

"He lives for stuff like that," Dillon had once said.

"Better get started, Maeve." Maeve almost jumped out of her seat. Mr. Sherman's voice was so deep and scary. Why couldn't he sound like one of those chipmunks that sing holiday songs? Maybe that would lighten everything up and she could relax.

He handed her the test, which looked like it had been kidnapped by packing tape fanatics. The Crow had wrapped so much tape around the envelope that Maeve would need ten pairs of scissors to free the test. Did he actually think she was going to cheat on her way to the study room? She was suddenly furious. She might be math-impaired, but she was no cheater.

Gathering up her notebook, Maeve felt as if she was crossing the Sahara Desert, her throat was so parched. She dug out a water bottle from her backpack, took a big swig, and hurried out of the room and down the hall to the library where someone would supervise her.

She got to work and she tried, she really tried. Matt had told her not to spend too much time on one problem. Skip it and come back to it later. Go through and work all the easy problems, answer the easy questions, then start back and try the harder ones.

The problem was there were no easy problems, no easy questions. She remembered to breathe like Matt told her, and she found a few she understood and worked those. She wasn't even halfway finished, though, when the buzzer made her jump and drop her pencil.

Ms. Curtis, the media librarian, walked over to where Maeve sat. "You have fifteen more minutes, Maeve, or even a half hour if you need it," she said. "Fortunately it's lunch time."

"I'm not even half finished," Maeve managed to say in a panicked voice. She wished she could vanish like a rabbit in a hat. Like Marty in the magic hat at the talent show. She wished she could run out the back of the school through a secret, hidden tunnel.

And at the mention of lunch, Maeve swallowed the lump rising from her stomach to her throat. She had to get away from this test. Feeling very weird, she shook her head, grabbed her things, and ran, leaving her test on her desk. Ms. Curtis could give it to Mr. Sherman. She didn't even know if she'd put her name on it, but he'd know it was hers. She had scribbled all in the margins. No one else in the class would turn in a half finished test.

She stopped short of running all the way to the office. Her heart was pounding, her breath coming in short panting huffs. *Please, please, don't let me faint in the hall. Let me be humiliated in private.*

"Maeve?" Ms. Sahni, Mrs. Fields' secretary, ran to help her as she stumbled into the office. "Are you sick?"

Maeve nodded her head. She pointed to Mrs. Fields' office door.

"Maybe the nurse's office would be a better place to go. You can lie down." Maeve could tell that Ms. Sahni was afraid that she was going to throw up, and that she wanted to turn Maeve over to the nurse rather than send her in to Mrs. Fields.

Maeve shook her head and pointed to the principal's door again. Fortunately, the door opened like magic, and Principal Fields stepped out.

"Why, Maeve, come in. Are you sick?" Mrs. Fields took one look at Maeve and knew something was very wrong.

Maeve nodded, walked past Mrs. Fields, and collapsed in a chair before she could faint dead onto the floor.

Mrs. Fields brought a cup of water and placed it before her. She watched as Maeve drank the entire cup. Then Maeve got out a tissue and mopped her head again.

"I—I—"

"Don't try to talk for a minute, Maeve. Just relax." Mrs. Fields closed her door, walked around, and sat in her desk chair. She gave Maeve another couple of minutes to compose herself and then began to talk softly.

"You know, Maeve, I am sitting here doing the budget for next semester. These figures are making my head swim. I can't make any sense of them. Would you like another glass of water?"

Maeve nodded. Her heart was slowing down and her throat was beginning to feel like normal. It must be the water, she thought. Avery told her once that water had amazing healing powers.

"Did you take your math test today, Maeve?"

Ruby Fields had been a junior high principal forever. She read kids' minds. Seldom did they actually have to tell her their problems. She knew before they spoke. She knew that Maeve struggled with math, that she had a math tutor, and that she had dyslexia, since she had been the one to give permission for Maeve to use a laptop in class.

Maeve nodded in between gulps of her "healing water." She promised herself she was going to start drinking more water every day. It couldn't hurt, she reasoned. Maybe, it would even help her with math.

"Yes, math tests can be very stressful sometimes. I can't tell you how many kids come in here worried about failing."

Maeve's eyes widened. She wasn't the only student who was freaking out about math. "Math makes me sick."

"The test made you sick? Or the idea that you may not have passed the test?" Mrs. Fields asked.

"Both. I'm sure I failed the test, Mrs. Fields. I didn't even get it finished, but I just couldn't work any longer. Does that mean I'm going to flunk seventh grade, that I have to take it over again next year? I'll just die if I have to stay back and all my friends go to eighth grade without me." Maeve slumped back in the chair.

✿

"I'm not sure it's gotten that dire, Maeve. I'm going to call both your parents and arrange a conference. Do you want me to have one of them come and get you, take you home for the rest of the day? How much sleep did you get last night?"

"Not much," Maeve admitted.

"Let's do that. You go home, have a nice nap, and see if you don't feel better. Then we'll find a time to talk at length, and see if we can't get to the root of this problem."

Maeve listened to Mrs. Fields call her mother. Part of her wanted to go home, part wanted to go to lunch with her friends. But she didn't think she could handle all of them asking her questions about the test and how she thought she did. Even though she was relieved to know that there were other kids who were bad at math, she was still embarrassed. No one likes to feel like they are at the bottom of the barrel, she sighed. Mrs. Fields suggested that she lie down on the couch and close her eyes for a while until her mother came. Maeve thought that was an excellent idea. When the principal placed a soft blanket over her, she felt relaxed for the first time in she didn't know how long. Katani was lucky to have such a sweet grandmother, Maeve thought, as her eyes began to shut.

"Maeve?" Ms. Kaplan looked in the door in what seemed like a very short time. "Sweetie, it's time to wake up. Are you all right?"

"I think Maeve would benefit by taking the rest of the day off, Ms. Kaplan. When you have a chance, could you give me a call? I'd like to arrange a conference with you and Maeve, her father, and Mr. Sherman. Let's see how we can work out this problem."

The word problem flashed larger than life for Maeve. She saw it in brilliant Technicolor spread across a movie marquee. *Problems with Maeve. Maeve and the Math Monster.*

Mother and Father Disown Daughter for Failing Math Test. One on One with "The Crow."

STAYING LOYAL

Katani found the BSG at their cafeteria table. She flopped down, set her tray before her, and sighed.

"The math test made Maeve sick." Katani took the lid off her cup of strawberry yogurt.

"How do you know that? Maybe she just went to the library," a concerned Charlotte offered.

"I'm sure. I saw Ms. Kaplan come and get Maeve from the office. Looks as if she's going home for the afternoon."

"Made her sick?" Avery said. "Really sick?"

"Well, she's going home isn't she? People don't get to go home in the middle of the day unless they are sick. What can we do?" Isabel asked.

It was so Isabel to want to help, Katani realized. She gave her friend a quick smile.

"I hope she can come to the sleepover tonight," Charlotte said. "The evening won't be the same without her."

Dillon and Nick stopped at their table. "Where is Maeve?" Dillon asked. "Is she still taking her test?"

"Her mother came and got her. She had to go home early." No way was Katani going to reveal that her friend freaked out about a math test and had to go home to get it together.

"Tell her I'll call her tomorrow," Dillon said. The two boys walked away. Mr. Popular stopped to chat at practically every table.

"Whoa, I wish we could tell Maeve right now that Dillon is going to call her tomorrow. She'd feel better immediately," Charlotte said. "Did you notice that Nick didn't say he'd call me tomorrow?"

✿

"Bet he will, though," Isabel teased.

"He has hardly spoken to me all week!" Charlotte was beginning to wonder if Nick liked her any more.

"Maybe he was studying. I think a lot of kids get freaked out by math tests," Isabel said. "Maeve more than anyone, but I get nervous, too."

"I was up late studying. I hope I won't fall asleep during our sleepover," Charlotte said.

"We can find something fun to do." Avery took a bite of her chicken and avocado wrap. "Maybe we can think of a new project."

"Or decide what clothes to wear to the—" Katani stopped herself.

"To the party, Katani," Avery said. "That's all right. You can talk about it. I'm over it."

"I can't go to the party either, Avery ... I have to take over a baby-sitting job for Elena ... She has a date."

"Baby-sit ... I can think of lots of things I'd rather do than baby-sit, but I do like to make some money. The Sports Locker has the coolest new basketball sneakers. Don't forget, Izzy, today is the second day of basketball tryouts."

"I know. I've been almost as worried about that as I was the math test."

"BSG, I have an idea," Katani said as they were gathering lunch clutter and getting ready to leave the cafeteria. "We've got to help Maeve with her math. What if she's right? What if flunking math would keep her back in seventh grade for another year?"

"No way." Avery shook her head. "Can they do that?"

"*They* can do anything they like," Katani said. "I think it'd be up to her parents and my grandmother, but she's struggling with all her work. We have to help her."

"But, how?" Charlotte asked. "I like math, it comes easy to me but I think I could help her more with writing."

"We have to make math fun," Katani announced.

"Fun?" Avery finally said. "I don't think there are too many people, except those super math geek geniuses, who think math is fun."

"What does Maeve like best, do best?" Katani asked.

"Sings, acts, dances, remembers old movies." Charlotte had gotten out her notebook and made a list as they talked.

"So we turn math into singing, dancing, and maybe even old movies." Katani made it sound simple.

"OK, and ...?" Isabel shrugged. "Do you know how to do that?"

"No, but there must be a way. Let's look on the Internet. There is an answer for everything there." Katani jumped up and clapped her hands. "Your assignment, BSG, should you accept it, is by tonight to think of ways to make math fun and easy and in some form that will stick in Maeve's mind."

"Maeve is smart," Charlotte said. "Let's try."

"Remember BSG rule no. 3: *we'll be loyal to our friends and won't lie to them even if they make a mistake or do something totally embarrassing,* like flunk math. One of the most important," said Isabel.

The Beacon Street Girls left with puzzled faces. How could they make math fun for their smart, math-phobic friend?

CHAPTER 6

MAKING MATH EASY IS HARD

"ARE YOU GOING to eat that piece of chicken, Maeve?" Sam asked with a hopeful look.

"Maybe. But you'd better not eat after me. I have the West Nile virus."

"Then I'm sure you have to stay home." Ms. Kaplan smiled at her dramatic daughter.

"Here, Sam, you can have my chicken."

"You are not going to Charlotte's without eating," her mom said.

Maeve popped a piece of chicken in her mouth.

When Maeve finished her chicken and salad, she was still hungry. She jumped up, looked in the fridge, and found one of her favorites—strawberry cheesecake flavored yogurt. "I'm going to eat this for dessert while I change clothes."

"Can I have your piece of cherry pie?" Sam yelled after Maeve to make sure she heard him.

"Geesh!" Maeve was glad she was going to get out of this house with her pesky, brainiac brother, who seemed to be inhaling all her food.

She put on a warmup suit over a pink long-sleeved T-shirt.

Quickly she stuffed pajamas, lotion, and, reluctantly, her notebook and math book into her overnight bag. Then she started up her laptop to check if the rest of the BSG had left for Charlotte's yet.

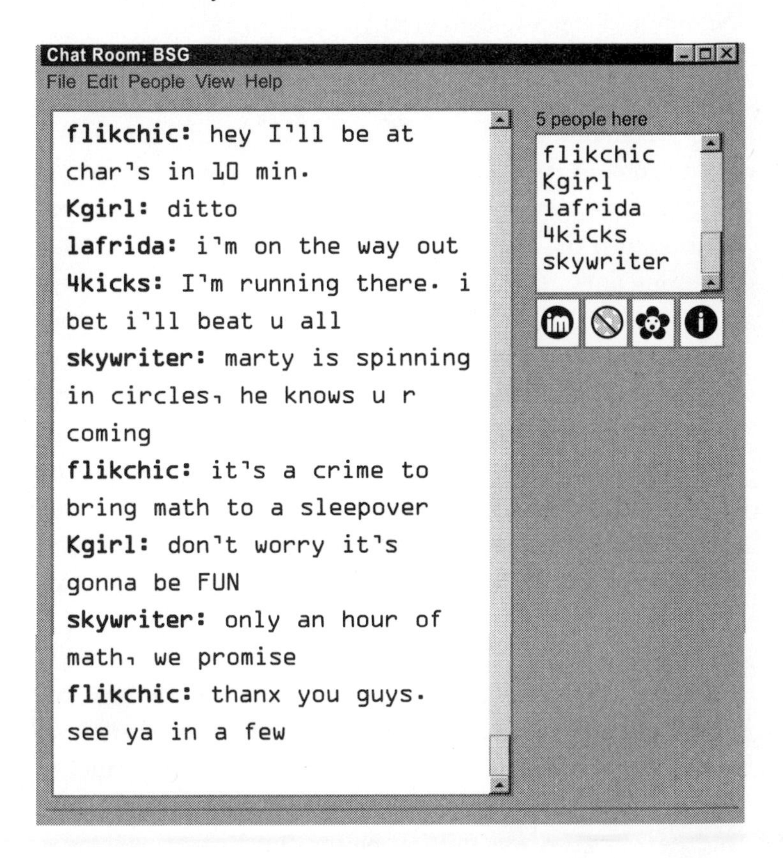

The plan was for the BSG to help her understand math tonight. If Maeve had her choice, she would rather play music and dance. Instead, she was actually spending a free night on math. The test was history … at least until they got

✿

their scores. The BSG were awfully nice to offer to help. *And who knows?* Maeve thought as she twisted her hair into a hair clip, maybe they could actually help her pass a makeup test. Ms. Kaplan dropped Maeve off, which was good, since Maeve didn't feel like walking. She was sure that she would perk up the minute she got to the Tower with her friends.

"Maeve, so, are you all right? We were so worried about you." Katani didn't wait for an answer and instead handed Maeve a handful of Swedish Fish. "I'm surprised your mother let you come, but we would have rescued you if she hadn't."

"Yeah, it's time for all of us to be together and catch up." Charlotte led the way from her room up to the Tower. "Did you bring any music?"

"Of course. You're going to love it." Maeve felt like a new person. She was thrilled that her friends wanted to dance. Dancing made you forget all your troubles. Even Avery, who originally resisted the idea of dancing at their sleepovers, had come around. "Dancing," she proclaimed, "was almost as good as bowling." The BSG had laughed so hard at that, but Avery insisted that she was not kidding. "Bowling is cool." Was there any sport that Avery didn't like? wondered Maeve.

Katani turned up the CD and the BSG began to shake it up. Maeve danced on an old couch with Marty, who seemed to like the music. He even barked to the beat once or twice. Isabel went spinning around the room while Katani rocked back and forth. Katani was still uncertain about her dancing skills, even when she was in front of her best friends. Maeve told her that she was getting better. But Katani, who was confident about her schoolwork and her fashion sense, felt completely incompetent about dancing. Slow and steady was her motto and not even Maeve's urging to "breakaway" could influence her to change.

"OK." Avery took charge. "Are we just going to relax and have fun, or should we stick with our plan to help Maeve?"

"You are helping me. Look how happy I am," she exclaimed as she executed a wild dance step that left the other BSG with their mouths hanging open.

"And the Best Dance Video Routine goes to ... drum roll, please ... Maeve Kaplan-Taylor," announced Isabel. "Take a bow, Ms. Kaplan-Taylor,"

"And then pull out your math book," added Charlotte with a wry smile.

Maeve's happy smile turned into a sad clown face.

"You can't fake us out Maeve. We have a mission to complete and we are all on it," Avery said as she slid off the Lime Swivel, their vintage salon chair.

Maeve laughed without much enthusiasm. She knew her friends meant well, but she wanted to forget school for the evening. "I vote for relaxing for a while."

"Anything we do together will be fun." Isabel poured everyone a cup of lemonade.

Katani stood up—a clipboard in her hand. "OK, team BSG. Find a comfortable place and listen up." Isabel, Maeve, Charlotte, and Avery scrambled to find their favorite Tower spot. Charlotte settled on the window seat. Maeve flung herself across the rug and plumped a pillow under her head. Avery scooted back into the Lime Swivel, while Isabel snuggled down next to Marty, who had fallen asleep on his favorite pillow. Four pairs of intent eyes turned to Katani who looked very much like the executive in charge.

"OK, BSG, I did a web search and found out some really interesting things about math and why some kids do really badly. I think the best way to tell you is to ask questions. Maeve, pay attention 'cause I think you might be surprised."

✿

Maeve stopped twirling the fringe on the pillow and focused on what Katani would ask. She hoped it wouldn't be one of those math questions where the answer was obvious to everyone but her. She hated that. It made her feel so stupid.

"Is your math teacher friendly and supportive?"

The girls hooted at that one. "The Crow, friendly and supportive. I don't think so. He can't even get my name straight," Maeve huffed.

"I guess the answer is no?" Katani looked at Maeve.

"Oh, yeah," Maeve waved her head back and forth. "I like this kind of test. Ask another question."

Katani smiled. This was going just as she hoped. She had found out that a lot of math problems occur because certain people who are nervous about math need a very supportive atmosphere to learn math.

"Does your teacher embarrass you in class in front of your classmates?"

Maeve jumped up. "The Crow is so mean. He makes me go to the board to do problems that he knows I can't do." She started pacing around the room like a cat on a fence.

"But, Maeve. Mr. Sherman asks everyone to go to the board. I don't think he wants to embarrass you. He just wants everyone to see the different ways a problem can mess up," said Avery.

Maeve couldn't believe her ears. "Are you defending him?"

Avery blinked. "Well. I mean, he is kind of weird and everything, but he isn't that bad of a teacher, really."

"What do you think, Isabel?"

Isabel hesitated. "Well, I think he is OK, but definitely kind of geeky, which makes it kind of hard to pay attention sometimes. I keep thinking that maybe he will really turn into a crow and start flying around the room." Isabel spoke so earnestly that her friends started to laugh. Maeve began flapping her arms like a bird while Avery let out a "caw."

Katani tapped her clipboard for order.

"Katani, what's the point of these questions?" Charlotte asked. A grateful Katani nodded to her friend. "I'm glad you asked that question. The problem isn't with you, Maeve, or Mr. Sherman. It has to do with the fact that some people like you need a quiet, supportive place to do math 'cause you have math anxiety. Avery and Isabel are OK in the class 'cause they don't get really nervous about math and you do."

"So all I need is a quiet room with a really nice teacher who doesn't make me feel stupid."

"Well, it's probably not that simple, but I bet that would help. Maybe you could talk to my grandmother about this. Now, did each of you bring a story problem, like I suggested?" Katani asked.

Four heads nodded and they dug in their notebooks for the problems. "I hate story problems," Maeve groaned, "They're so useless."

"These aren't. That was the idea." Avery spread out her folded sheet of paper. "Here's mine. Isabel will help me read. I'm the movie manager." Avery cleared her throat and lowered her voice to sound important. "Maeve, you have to go to work at 10:35 a.m. today. You have to work two hours and fifteen minutes before you can have a break."

Isabel read. "Ring-ring. That's your cell phone, Maeve."

"I don't have my cell phone with me," Maeve said.

"Pretend you do. Ring-ring. Hello, Maeve, this is Dillon. What time can you go to lunch with me today?"

"Dillon has never called and invited me out to lunch." Maeve sighed. "I wish he would."

"Today he has. What time can you go?" Charlotte handed

✿

Maeve a pencil, since she didn't seem to have one.

Maeve sighed again. "OK. At least figuring this out makes sense. 10:35 to 11:35 is one hour. 11:35 to 12:35 is two hours. Fifteen minutes?" She scribbled a little. 12:50. Ten minutes till one. We'll both be starved. Hello, Dillon. I can go to lunch at 12:50. Is that too late?"

Charlotte laughed. Maeve was so funny and endearing sometimes without even meaning to be. Before they could think up another math problem, Maeve stood up. "I here and now declare that we won't do any more studying tonight. Let's do something fun. I want to forget school."

"What do you suggest?" Avery said.

"Well, earlier I called my dad. I asked him if we got bored would it be all right to come to the horror festival movie."

"Horror festival? Awesome," Katani said. "I love scary horror movies."

"What's playing?" Charlotte asked. "I probably haven't seen anything he has on the schedule."

"Tonight is *Bride of Frankenstein*." Maeve made her voice spooky, and then paraded down the aisle as if she had a bouquet of flowers.

"I think Ole Frank would be more attracted to someone who walked like this." Avery walked across the room like a stiff robot. Everyone laughed and agreed.

"I can't see Frankenstein hip hop dancing, can you?" Isabel laughed. She had seen *Frankenstein* so many times that it didn't scare her anymore.

"Let's go!" Maeve pulled on her warmup and looked at her watch. "We can just make it in time."

The girls dashed out of the house, waving good-bye to a startled Mr. Ramsey, who'd been visiting with Miss Pierce.

"Off to the movie, Dad. Back in a couple." Charlotte

called out her plans.

They ran, while Maeve occasionally danced down the hill toward the movie theater. Maeve chased after Isabel, screaming in her best Wicked Witch of the West imitation, "I'll get you my pretty!"

"Hurry," Maeve's dad said to them as they poured into the theater. "The guys are saving you seats about halfway down in the middle."

"The guys?" Charlotte laughed. "Maeve, you didn't? You planned this all along, didn't you?"

"They could have watched the movie without us if you had said no, or insisted we study. We can't study all the time in the Tower. It's sacred. It should be reserved only for fun and oh-so-important BSG meetings."

Maeve led the way. The theater was already dark and showing previews. She blinked her eyes and tried to see. She didn't want to fall over someone's legs or sit in a lap.

"Maeve," Dillon whispered. "Over here. Hurry, we had trouble saving the seats."

The theater was crowded, and some people seemed annoyed when a pack of very late, laughing girls tumbled into their seats.

Nick passed popcorn from one end of the row, and Dillon picked up Cokes from the floor one by one from the other end. Maeve had told Dillon to bring anyone else he wanted, as long as it wasn't too many.

Pete Wexler, Josh and Billy Trentini had held seats in the middle. They stayed together. But as soon as the spooky movie started, all eyes were glued to the screen. No talking, but gasps, little screams, and giggles were allowed.

Maeve always had to wipe tears from her eyes when Frankenstein tried to convince his inventor he was lonely.

His face was ugly, but so sad. She understood how he felt.

They sat through a few credits at the end, letting other people leave the movie first. Then Nick led the way out of their row. "That was classic," he said.

"That was great, Maeve," Charlotte said. "Thank you."

"I love horror movies." Maeve looked at Dillon. "Don't you, Dillon?"

"I think Frankenstein would have made a good basketball player. That would have made him happy."

"He'd have had to limber up a little," Avery said. "But he was tall enough."

"Who's ready for pizza?" Nick asked.

"Or nachos," Dillon suggested. "Let's go to Anna's."

"Let's vote." Avery looked around, counting the scores. "It's pizza."

Village Fare was small, but luckily not too crowded. They moved tables together until they all could sit at one big one.

"Our treat, girls, since Maeve treated for the movie." Nick collected money from the boys and ordered three pizzas. "We'll order another if we're running out."

"Do you really believe Frankenstein got lonely?" Pete asked.

"Why not? Monsters have feelings." Maeve never once doubted that Frankenstein needed a bride. She thought it was sweet of Pete to ask.

Conversation flew around the table about the movie, then moved to sports, school, teachers, and inevitably to the party.

Avery didn't know whether to be quiet and listen or protest and start another conversation. She realized any mention of the party bothered her, even when she'd resolved it wouldn't. She threw out the idea of Frankenstein playing basketball with the Crow. Soon they were laughing so much, they could hardly eat.

It was a good way to put a finish to the evening, their own impromptu movie and pizza party. Maeve was happy.

CHAPTER 7

FAMILY DAY

WHEN MAEVE got home from Charlotte's the next morning, she was feeling much more like her old self. She opened the door to immediately hear the sound of a vacuum. Uh-oh, her mother was on one of her cleaning rampages. When Ms. Kaplan cleaned, everyone cleaned.

"Hi, Maeve," her mother said, shutting off the noise so they could talk. "Did you have fun?" She didn't even wait for Maeve's answer. "I need you to clean your room and then the afternoon is yours. Don't set that down there! Take it to your room."

Maeve clutched her favorite *Think Pink* overnight bag to her chest. "Can we go shopping this afternoon? I need something new, even one thing, for the party next weekend." Maeve wasn't sure this was a good time to ask her mother for a favor, but her mother was so busy during the week, there didn't seem to be very many times when she was available.

"Well, I could use one new outfit for work. And you're so good at picking out clothes that look good on me. But I don't think I'll have time today. I have to do the laundry, finish cleaning the kitchen, go grocery shopping, and make some lasagna and meat loaf for dinner next week. Maybe I can pick you up one day after school. I just can't believe how I've let everything here go."

Hoping for the best, Maeve cleaned her room, cleaned the guinea pig cage, and made lunch for her mother and Sam. She had to admit that she felt bad for her mother, who never seemed to have any free time anymore.

After lunch, she called around, but no one was home. Katani was shopping with her mom and sister Kelley. Charlotte and her dad had gone to the Aquarium. Avery was playing basketball, probably shooting hoops with Dillon. Maeve wasn't jealous, since she knew Avery and Dillon were only friends. Avery had a knack for making friends with boys. Maybe it was because they all had sports in common. Isabel said she had to help her mother do her physical therapy today.

OK, that settles it! I'll go practice my dance moves, Maeve thought. She had way too much energy left, and if they weren't going shopping, she had to find a way to use it up.

As she entered her room, a rustling sound from her closet made her curious. She looked at Elle and Bruiser. No, they hadn't gotten loose. Maeve had made sure the door to their cage was secure after she'd cleaned. She reached for the closet door.

"Aiiiii!" Sam screamed and jumped out at Maeve. He leaped into a Tae Kwon Do pose and challenged her to fight.

Maeve fell back onto her bed. "Sam, oh, Sam. You gave me a heart attack. What are you doing?"

"I'm Cato. You know, from the *Pink Panther* movies. You know how—"

Maeve took a deep breath. "Yes, I know, Sam. Inspector Clouseau's Asian manservant jumps out at him. But you're the one taking Tae Kwon Do, not me. I don't need to practice with you. Don't ever do that again, you hear? I almost jumped out of my skin!"

"Really? That's neat." Sam took off running down the stairs. "Aiiiiii!"

Annoying little brothers! Maeve crawled up into bed with her laptop and stared at the ceiling of her room until she decided what she wanted to say.

Notes to Self:

1. Consider asking Dad to take Sam and let me live alone with Mom.
2. Practice some of the BSG story problems again ... or not. I won't say that they're fun, but the BSG are fun, and they thought up the problems, so these problems are fun by association.
3. Make thank you cards for the BSG ... maybe scented? A different scent for each?
4. Tomorrow is Family Day—Mom's new kick on family time, with all four of us. Sam and I take turns deciding what to do each Sunday.
5. Get outfit ready for Sam's Tae Kwon Do.

SUNDAY

"It's my day to choose," Sam said at breakfast.

"Yes it is." Mom was looking through the cupboards and making a list. "It would have been your day no matter what. You're getting your yellow belt."

"He hopes he's getting his yellow belt," Maeve pointed out. "And if going around the house jumping in the air, kicking an invisible assailant, and yelling 'Aiiiii!' will help, he's ready."

"I scared you, didn't I?"

"Yeah, well, next time I'm getting my black belt so you better watch out." Maeve poured herself some orange juice. She'd eat something in a minute.

"Maeve, let Sam have some fun." Ms. Kaplan sipped a cup of coffee. She had a funny look on her face. Was she dreading Family Day, spending time with Maeve's father?

"Whatever." Maeve took her orange juice to her room. She took a shower and dressed quickly in her best jeans and a hot pink tee. She threaded a colorful scarf into the loops of her jeans as a belt. She applied a glob of styling gel to her hair until it was a shining fountain of fire. Hey, that was good, she preened, kind of a rock star look—big and poofy. She liked having wild red hair. Inspired, Maeve grabbed the tube of toothpaste and pretended she was the newest *American Idol* winner. She shook her head, tossed her hair back, and began dancing and singing around the room. Suddenly, Sam burst in, his hands over his ears screaming, "Make it stop!"

Maeve picked up her pillow and threw it at him. Sam started to laugh hysterically.

"What's so funny?"

He was laughing so hard he couldn't even speak, so he pointed at her hair. Maeve dropped the tube of toothpaste and ran to look in the mirror. Her hair had gone wild. It was as if she had been electrocuted. Maeve did what any self respecting 12 year old would do in her situation … she screamed.

Hearing the ear piercing scream, her mother came running into the room.

"What is going on here?"

Maeve stormed out of the bathroom, grasping at her hair. "Do you see this hair? It looks like a fright wig!"

Ms. Kaplan was speechless. Her daughter's hair was three times the size it usually was. She had to bite the insides of her cheeks to keep from laughing. Maeve's hair looked so … so … atrocious.

Collecting herself, Ms. Kaplan gave her daughter a hug and told her to tie her hair back because they were leaving shortly. She ordered Sam out of his sister's room and told him to stop "tormenting your sister."

When they left the room. Maeve went back into the bathroom to stare at her crowning glory. Even she had to laugh. She wished the BSG were there to see their friend Maeve starring in a remake of *Bride of Frankenstein*.

Maeve carefully combed her red mop down, wrapped it into a knot on top of her head, letting a couple of tendrils stay loose as if by accident. This was a good style. Casual, as if she didn't care if it was a little bit messy. Hair was definitely more interesting than math. Maybe she could go to hairdresser's school in case the acting/dancing thing didn't work out. She could see herself creating dramatic hairstyles for celebrity parties and weddings. "Hair by Maeve"… it had a certain ring to it. Of course, she wouldn't make much money unless it was her own business, and to have your own business you needed to understand math. Maeve sighed. She couldn't even get away from math in her own dreams.

She rummaged through her jewelry box for her favorite pair of dangly earrings. She hoped she could talk to Riley soon about singing with his band again.

She fed Elle and Bruiser two pellets of guinea pig chow each. "I'll play with you some night this week, guys," she said. "There just isn't time left today since I slept so late. Sorry, but at least you have a clean cage."

The two guinea pigs gave a squeak. Sometimes, Maeve was sure those little pigs were psychic. They understood everything she said to them, and sometimes things she didn't say.

"Are you ready, Maeve?" her mother called. "Your father is picking us up at 11:00." Her hair finally presentable, Maeve went to the kitchen to grab a bagel. Her mother walked into the kitchen wearing a big smile and clothes that Maeve had never seen her wear before.

"What do you think, sweetheart?"

"Mom! You look great. Those jeans are hip and that turquoise tee looks great with that jacket. When did you get so stylish? You look like a mom on a sitcom."

The colors made her mom look really pretty. As did her new hair style and hoop earrings. She looked, well, she looked happy for a change. And Maeve wondered why … could there be a man in her mother's life that she didn't know about?

"Mom?"

"What, sweetie?" she asked as she took a sip of her coffee.

"What am I going to do if I flunked that math test … I know I did."

"Your father and I have already talked about it. We have a meeting scheduled with Ruby Fields and Mr. Sherman. I'm going to ask Matt to sit in on the conference with us. We'll work something out."

"He's here, he's here." Sam dashed into the kitchen, jumped into the air, and kicked a chair over. He didn't mean to kick the chair—that was just where his foot hit when it flew out. *Bam*!

"Sam, please." Ms. Kaplan groaned. "Save all that energy for your test."

"Yeah, I'm going to get my yellow belt today and then work really hard and move up fast. I'll have a black belt by the time I'm ten."

Maeve shook her head. "I have to brush my teeth again, Mom. Only take me a minute." She chugged the rest of her hot chocolate, dashed out of the kitchen, and raced up the stairs. You never did know who you might run into at a Tae Kwon Do school.

"Carol, you look lovely," Mr. Taylor said when they were tucked into the car and ready to roll.

"Why thank you, Ross." Ms. Kaplan looked out the window, but from right behind her, Maeve could see a tiny smile on her face.

Her mother and father were being weird. Her mother was acting like—well, like a high school girl. Maeve looked at Sam, who shrugged. Grownups were so impossible to figure out sometimes. Maeve wondered: Could it be that the new man in her mother's life was ... her dad? That would be just too weird.

The Tae Kwon Do school was so crowded, Maeve's mom grabbed her hand to keep them together. Sam seemed to know where to go. He took off running in a different direction before anyone could stop him.

"Sam, come back here!" Maeve's mother shouted.

"Don't worry, Mom. If Sam gets lost, he'll wander around until he finds his class. Unless he jumps out and surprises someone and gets stomped."

Next time Sam pulled that trick on her, she was going to let loose with her best *King Kong* lady in distress scream. That should teach him a lesson.

In Maeve's eyes, the gym was a blur of kids dressed in white Tae Kwon Do uniforms, all looking alike. Except that there were different sizes of white-suited people from little munchkins like Sam to, to, hey, teenaged boys. Interspersed were a few teenaged girls, but not many.

She wondered how hard it was to get good at Kung Fu. Maybe if she got her black belt she could add it to her resume and get movie parts that would take her on location to Korea or China or Japan. How exotic! Maeve Kaplan-Taylor, Tomb Raider. Ready to enter the Temple of Doom and save the priceless antique samurai swords of the ancient Bengal hoards. She'd have on khaki shorts and a pink shirt with the sleeves rolled up. Couldn't wear sequins or they'd sparkle and give away her hiding places. But she'd have stylish, lace-up boots and pink socks. And maybe she would save orphans for the United Nations and help with tsunami kinds of things. Maybe she could win a humanitarian award. That would be nice. Her parents had been so proud of her when she won an award for making blankets for the Jeri's Place homeless shelter. The thought that helping someone is better than getting straight As in math made her feel slightly better about the whole test fiasco.

Maeve followed her mother and father up into the bleachers. She hoped they weren't going to sit there forever. The Tae Kwon Do people should be showing a Karate Kid movie or Jackie Chan flick for people who had to wait around all day.

"Did anyone get a program?" Maeve asked. She had already realized she couldn't sit there for hours with her parents. They were whispering like teenagers. And her mother was giggling. Giggling! And totally ignoring her. Boy, was this weird.

"What time is Sam's group going on? I don't think I can sit here much longer."

Her father looked at the program. "Best I can figure, it might be another hour or more before his group tests." Dad dug in his pocket. "Here, Maeve, why don't you go see if you can find us something to eat? I didn't have any breakfast."

"Ross, you didn't eat breakfast?"

"A cup of coffee. I forgot to get groceries. And I usually go out for breakfast before the first matinee."

Maeve took the fistful of dollar bills. "I'll try, but I don't have too much hope of finding anything."

She could spend an hour looking around. And once Sam did his thing, they'd leave and get a late lunch. Her father was definitely in a good mood. He was enjoying her mother's company. A big smile escaped onto Maeve's face.

She stuffed the money into her tote bag and stepped down the bleachers into a sea of buzzing white outfits. Like snow bees. Was there any such thing as snow bees? Maeve Kaplan-Taylor, explorer, in search of the elusive snow bees on the slopes of Mount Kilimanjaro.

That sounded like a good plot, and a fun place to go on location. Unless she actually had to climb the mountain. Maybe there were chairlifts.

In a couple of minutes, she went from being an explorer/tomb raider to feeling a little uneasy. There were about a million guys there. Two boys her age stopped to talk to her.

"Are you testing today?" a boy with red hair almost the shade of hers smiled at her.

"What belt do you have?" Red's friend had the kind of blue eyes you only read about or saw in the movies.

"She's not testing today," another boy said. His teeth were covered with metallic blue braces. "Can't you see she's not dressed for testing? Do you have a red belt already? Black? No, you couldn't have a black belt."

"I—I—" This was more boy attention than even she was used to.

Just smile and keep your cool. This is how it will be everywhere you go when you're a famous actress or rock star. You can do it.

"Has—does anyone know where I can get something to drink?" She stuttered when she asked, but she smiled to make up for it.

"Maeve, hey, Maeve, what are you doing here?" A familiar voice called to her. She reached out for the speaker like he was a lifesaver ring tossed to her while drowning and surrounded by big white sharks.

"Dillon? Dillon is that you? I didn't know you were taking Tae Kwon Do."

Either he was, or he'd dressed in white pants so he'd fit in. His smiling face was terribly welcome. And when he took her arm and pulled her off to the side, away from that crush of admirers, she could have hugged him. She didn't, of course. She would never want to embarrass him like that.

✿

"Yeah, I'm going for my red belt today. Want to come and watch?"

Maeve looked at Dillon. She thought basketball was his only interest. Dillon ... Riley ... just when you think you know someone, they go and surprise you.

"If you want to come," Dillon invited again, "we have to hurry."

"I-oh-yes, but I'll have to tell my parents where I am. We're here to watch Sam get his yellow belt."

"That's after my test. You'll have plenty of time."

Maeve took off to find her parents again and tell them where she was. "Mom, Dad, I found Dillon here. He wants me to watch his exam."

"How do you always find someone you know when we go somewhere?" her mother asked.

"She's outgoing, Carol." Her father smiled at Maeve. "Just like you were in school. Go ahead, Maeve, but be sure you get back to watch Sam's test."

"I have a program. I will, I promise."

Maeve took off, making sure not to run and look too eager. But she didn't want Dillon to be late. He grabbed her hand, and they took off to another open area of the high school building. Dillon pointed to bleachers. "If you sit close to that mat, you can see."

He got in line behind a class of boys and one girl about his age. Only once, before he went on the mat, did he look up, smile, and wave. Then he became someone she didn't know.

He bowed to the mat, to his teacher, then in front of someone with a clipboard and pen. The teacher put Dillon through a series of moves. He kicked out in front, spun, and kicked in back. He made a whole string of precise moves, holding poses, jumping into new stances. His technique was similar to what Sam had been trying to do all over the house, except that Dillon looked almost professional, like the Karate Kid, but taller.

Maeve had never seen Dillon so serious. Never once did he look up and wave or smile at her. His mind was totally focused—not the goofy cutup he was in school.

He moved on to sparring, being assigned an opponent. The teacher watched as the two boys moved precisely. It seemed to be up to Dillon's opponent to protect himself. As he threw a punch, he yelled "Aiiiii," just like Sam had been doing as Cato. The boy would fight back, they'd slide across the mat fighting, then chop with the side of a hand. There were probably names for the moves, but Maeve had no idea what they were. She just knew that Dillon was good, as were each of the boys he fought against. She was glad he didn't fight with the girl, although once she took her eyes off Dillon to watch her for a few seconds. She seemed to be holding her own.

When they were finished, there was a ceremony. Dillon walked up to his teacher and bowed. The teacher pulled off Dillon's blue belt and tied the red belt around his waist. Dillon bowed again. The class stood at the edge of the mat watching until each person got a new belt. Maeve was so glad. Flunking in front of this crowd of parents and friends would have been too embarrassing.

Dillon stepped off the mat, bowed a final time, then hurried over to where she sat. "What did you think, Maeve? Want to take lessons?"

"Fabulous, Dillon. I had no idea you could do that."

"It's not something I talk about a lot. This is kind of ... you know ... private." Maeve was surprised at how serious Dillon's voice sounded.

"Thank you for letting me watch." Dillon had shared an

intriguing side of himself Maeve might never have known about had she not run into him. She felt kind of special.

"I'll go with you to watch Sam," Dillon offered.

"OK. Do you ever teach the younger kids?"

"I'm ready to do that now. I wanted to get my red belt first."

"Is black next?"

"Yes, first degree black, then there are more advanced degrees. I'll stay with it and go as far as I can." Maeve could see it now. Dillon and Maeve in Hollywood. Mr. and Mrs. Kung Fu.

Dillon held out his hand and together they ran back to where Sam was going to test at one end of a big gym.

"Look, Mom, Dad, Dillon got his red belt," Maeve said. "It was awesome to watch. Much different from a karate movie. We came back to watch Sam. Is he up next?"

"Almost. Come up here and sit down," her father said. "Talk to me, Dillon. Tell me why you decided to take a martial arts class. What do you think? You think an old guy like me could take this sport on?"

Maeve looked at her mother. Mom shrugged, smiled, and then hugged Maeve to her while Dad and Dillon visited. Maeve was glad for her father to get to know Dillon. She was glad to learn something she didn't know about Dillon. Maybe he was two people, the goofy guy who teased her all the time, who loved the cheers from the Abigail Adams basketball fans, and this poised, serious fighter guy.

She liked both.

Sam waved as he ran out to his mat to test. They watched him go through a scaled down version of Dillon's test. But Maeve could see something happening to Sam when he got on the floor and performed his moves for the tester. Sam was growing up a little bit. Maeve was proud of her pesky little brother. She'd tell him so when they got home.

Dad invited Dillon to go to lunch with them, but Dillon said his family was expecting him home.

Family. Maeve liked that word. She also liked the idea of Family Day, which had been surprisingly fun and not at all boring. And Maeve now had new hope that her own family would be back together again someday.

CHAPTER 8

BASKETBALL RULES!

CHARLOTTE HAD planned to meet Isabel in *The Sentinel* office before school on Monday. She was still polishing her feature article on the Lake Rescue experience, and Isabel needed to put finishing touches on two cartoons.

"Before I forget to tell you, Charlotte, Isabel ..." Jennifer Robinson, editor of the school newspaper said. "You two did a great job on the seventh-grade page. Ms. Knowland couldn't be here this early this morning, but she sends her congratulations. She said your idea, Charlotte, of having seventh-grade reporters was excellent." Jennifer pushed up her funky purple glasses and smiled.

"You're going to ask me to write something else, aren't you, Jen?" Charlotte said. She appreciated the compliment, but she was also suspicious of Jennifer's motives.

Jennifer grinned. "Uh-oh, you're getting to know me too well. That was fast. Riley said to tell you he couldn't have a music review done this time, and Maeve must have totally forgotten she said she'd have an 'Ask Maeve' column for this issue. Can you check with her on that? But no matter what, I need one more article from you, by tomorrow, about the trip in general. Just remember some things you did and an anecdote about each. Not a thought piece, like your feature, which is terrific. I read it this morning."

"But, Jen, I'm not finished with it. I have more to add, and I haven't corrected it yet." Charlotte was dismayed that Jennifer had read an unfinished piece of writing. She liked people to see her best work. It made her feel uncomfortable to turn in something that wasn't proofed.

"That's OK. You have good last-minute changes. That's why I know you can write this article by tomorrow. It's great practice for working on a newspaper." Jennifer hurried to her desk, piled high with work. Her in-basket overflowed, and empty cans of soda littered the entire desk.

"I don't think I want to be a newspaper reporter, Isabel," Charlotte said in a low voice. "But maybe she's right. I need to learn to write faster."

"Good luck. The more pressure someone puts on me to draw something, the more I panic. I can't work at all. I have to be relaxed and happy to create. I'm very right brained, you know?"

"Hi, Charlotte, Isabel." Chelsea Briggs walked in with a handful of discs. "Do you have time to look at photos and help me choose? I took a ton of pictures at camp so I'd have choices, and now I can't choose. I've narrowed them down to ten, but Jennifer says I can have only two this week. Charlotte, you're the seventh-grade page editor. Maybe you can make room for three."

Isabel looked at Charlotte. Charlotte was sure her face reflected dismay at the load of work and only two days left to finish.

She could stay after school today and come in early

tomorrow and that was it. Unless ... she had library today, and maybe she could get out of gym.

Isabel chimed in. "I'll help you, Chelsea, if you look at three cartoons and give me suggestions. I'm like you, I can't choose, but in an emergency I could deliver them Wednesday morning."

Charlotte could have hugged Isabel for saving her. She hated to say no to Chelsea, who had really come out of her shell lately, but she had her own work to finish. One more rewrite would polish her feature. Charlotte was used to working on poetry where every word had to be perfect. And old habits die hard, the cliché goes. At least there wasn't time for any fear to wade through. *And the seventh-grade page was your idea,* a little voice reminded her. "Yeah, yeah." She smiled and started her computer.

WHO'S IN? WHO'S OUT?

Avery got through classes on Monday the way she usually did—laughing, joking, and giving Billy Trentini and his twin brother, Josh, a hard time. But underneath, she was about to burst. She was sure she'd made the basketball team, but ever since she had been excluded from Julie's party, she had started to feel that nothing was a sure thing anymore.

She'd have bet anything that Julie Faber would have invited her to her birthday party. Now she thought maybe Julie hated her. Just goes to show, you never know what other people are thinking and feeling, especially if they're really good fakers.

"Any news yet about the team, Avery?" Charlotte asked at lunch when all the BSG met at their table. "I'm sure your name will be at the top of the list."

"Numero uno." Isabel held up her finger.

"And you'll be numero dos," Avery countered. She knew a little bit of Spanish herself.

"Any number will suit me, as long as I make the team."

"What's the word for team in Spanish?" Avery asked.

"Equipo," Isabel said.

Equipo. As much as Avery loved sports and the BSG and Marty, she kind of liked words, too. She and Charlotte had that in common. She wasn't as creative with her writing as Charlotte, though. She preferred talking. She wished Abigail Adams had a debate team. She'd try out. If you were good with words, you could talk yourself in or out of anything, except maybe getting an invitation to the party of the year.

Avery bit her lip. She wanted to stop thinking about the party. But, a little voice in her head kept repeating Julie Faber, Julie Faber. It was weird how you could be feeling so good about yourself, and one person could totally ruin your mood. It wasn't fair.

Maybe she'd surprise Julie and everyone else by showing up anyway. She'd walk into the room and find the party was a total flop. No one would be talking, except for people whispering about what to do. Avery would hand Julie a stack of games, and pretty soon everyone would be laughing and saying, "What a great party." That Avery had saved the day. And Julie would come over to her and apologize. "I'm really sorry I didn't invite you in the first place, Avery, I'm sorry, I'm sorry ..."

"Earth to Avery. World to Avery. Come in, Avery." Katani reminded her she was at lunch. "What are you thinking about? Basketball tryouts? Why did I ask?"

Avery blinked once and shot back to Planet Earth. To cover her brief lapse, she pulled out a banana. "What's with the odd couple?" Avery asked, pointing to Anna, sitting beside the Yurtmeister, or was he sitting beside her?

"You never know about chemistry," Maeve answered. "Do you think Anna will go out with Henry? He keeps hanging out with her. Maybe he's hoping she'll get used to seeing him and give in to a date or something."

"Used to be Anna and Joline were so predictable, but these days I'm not so sure." Avery smiled. "But I think Anna will make the basketball team for sure. They're going to post names after school today in the gym. Want to go practice math cheers with Isabel and me after school, Maeve? While we wait for the news?"

"No, I don't want people to know I have to do that to learn math." Maeve looked at all of them. "Not that I don't appreciate your trying to help me, guys. I do, and the funny thing is, that story problem about Dillon inviting me to lunch is still in my head. And I keep thinking of more. I think I could work any story problem on a test easily. Why do you think that is?"

"We turned math into something you were interested in, Maeve." Charlotte laughed. "If we wrote a movie about how a right-angle girl fell in love with a square boy, got married, and together they made a triangle kid who rode a tricycle, you'd remember that."

"Yeah, tri means three. Do you think I could get Matt to use that technique?" Maeve looked perkier, ready to smile and be her old self. "We could call the movie *Romantic Equation*."

"Matt might be glad for you to have a breakthrough any way you can get it," Charlotte said.

Avery chugged the rest of the lime water she'd brought in her lunch sack. "Hey, Dillon," Avery called out. Dillon was returning his lunch tray. Nick Montoya walked beside him.

"Dude? Basketball team list out yet?"

"No. But I wondered how you did on your test. Did you get your red belt?"

"Ask Maeve." Dillon smiled. He pushed Nick, Nick pushed back. They sparred their way out of the lunch room.

"He did," Maeve said to Avery. "I watched him. How did you know that Dillon was taking Tae Kwon Do? And why didn't you tell me? I only saw him at the meet by accident. He seems to have kept the classes quiet."

"Maybe the subject just never came up, Maeve. You and Dillon need to sit and talk more instead of your just romanticking about him." Avery made a goofy face at Maeve.

"Romanticking? I love that word." Charlotte laughed.

"I'll think about that." Maeve smiled. "I could sit and talk to Dillon about Tae Kwon Do. Sam got his yellow belt. I was pretty amazed. He settled down the minute he got on the mat and was as polite to his teacher and his opponent as I've ever seen him."

"That's part of what they teach in self-defense classes, Maeve. Respect for your enemies," said Charlotte.

"Then you totally respect Julie Faber, Ave?" Katani asked.

"I really didn't know she was my enemy. If she makes the team, I'll play fair with her, but don't ask me to like her."

R-E-S-P-E-C-T

As soon as the last bell rang, Avery and Isabel raced each other to the gym. They approached the bulletin board where a crowd of seventh- and eighth-grade girls pushed and shoved, trying to see the list posted there. Avery kept her cool, but in her pocket, her fingers were crossed, and butterflies fluttered in her stomach. Instead of pushing and shoving like the crowd, Avery moved away. She took a deep breath and executed a few jumping jacks. On her last hop, Anna and

✿

Joline approached, looking as pleased with themselves as they usually did.

"How old are you, Avery?" Anna asked.

"Why do you want to know ... taking a survey?" Avery answered. The question sounded like a classic Anna and Joline setup.

"Well, in case you wanted to know, the reason you didn't get invited to the party of the year is because you are so immature. You act like you're still in grade school."

That did it. It was one thing not to be invited to Julie's party if Julie plain didn't like her. But it was another to be considered immature. Who did Julie think she was anyway? Just because she wore a ton of makeup and had a new crush every week, she thought *she* was mature?

Avery spun away from Anna and Joline. Did having a lot of energy, having fun, liking sports, all sports, make her immature? Anna's remark hurt. Did everyone in her grade think she was immature? Did the BSG?

"Avery." She spun around and stood up, only to find herself face to face with Julie Faber. Great, Avery fumed. A Fabulous Faber moment. Just what she needed now.

"I ... about my party ... I didn't think you'd want to come. You're always playing soccer or basketball, and I just didn't think you were into parties ... especially ones with dancing." Anna and Joline snickered behind her back.

Avery felt her face flush. She wasn't into partying? What she wasn't into was being left out when all her friends got invitations to something.

"You can come to the party if you want to, Avery. But I'm out of invitations. You can just look at Charlotte or Katani's invitation to get the info."

Look at her friends' invitations instead of getting one?

She didn't think so.

"No thanks, Julie. I have other plans. I'm going to a fundraiser." Avery crossed her fingers behind her back. Surely, her mother had some party she could tag along to. So she wasn't really lying.

"OK. Whatever." Julie walked away without saying more and headed toward the Queens of Mean, who were looking sidelong at Avery and laughing. Had they heard Julie invite her? Had they put her up to it just to see if she would come? Avery noticed she was standing almost in the middle of the gym all alone. The girls who hung around Julie were giggling and laughing. Were they laughing at her?

Avery realized she could be the victim of a cruel joke. It would have been better if Julie hadn't said anything, hadn't invited her at all. Avery felt like crying. Where was Isabel? Avery had to bite her lip to keep from going to pieces when Isabel finally walked up and put her hand on Avery's arm.

As everyone else was leaving, Isabel and Avery hurried over and stared at the names, but Avery had a little trouble reading through blurry eyes.

"You made the team, Avery. And wow, I'm there! Can you believe it?" Isabel jumped up and down. "I would never have tried out if you hadn't pushed me to do it, Ave. I'm going to practice every chance I get so I won't let you down."

"Let *me* down?" Avery sniffed and laughed. "How about Coach Porter and Abigail Adams Junior High? I'll help you work on your game."

Avery wiped her eyes, hoping Isabel wasn't watching. She wasn't, she was looking at the board again. "Hey, Ave, Betsy made the team. Julie made it. Anna, of course. I think the rest are eighth graders. They'll probably think we're *immature*, but we'll show them."

✿

Avery laughed. "Thanks, Izzy. I'm really glad you moved here ... even though you are so immature. Let's go to my house and get online. We need to tell Charlotte, Maeve, and Katani we're in."

No one was home at Avery's house. Her mother had left a note that she had gone to Scott's basketball game. The two girls settled at Avery's computer, while Avery brought up the IM chat room.

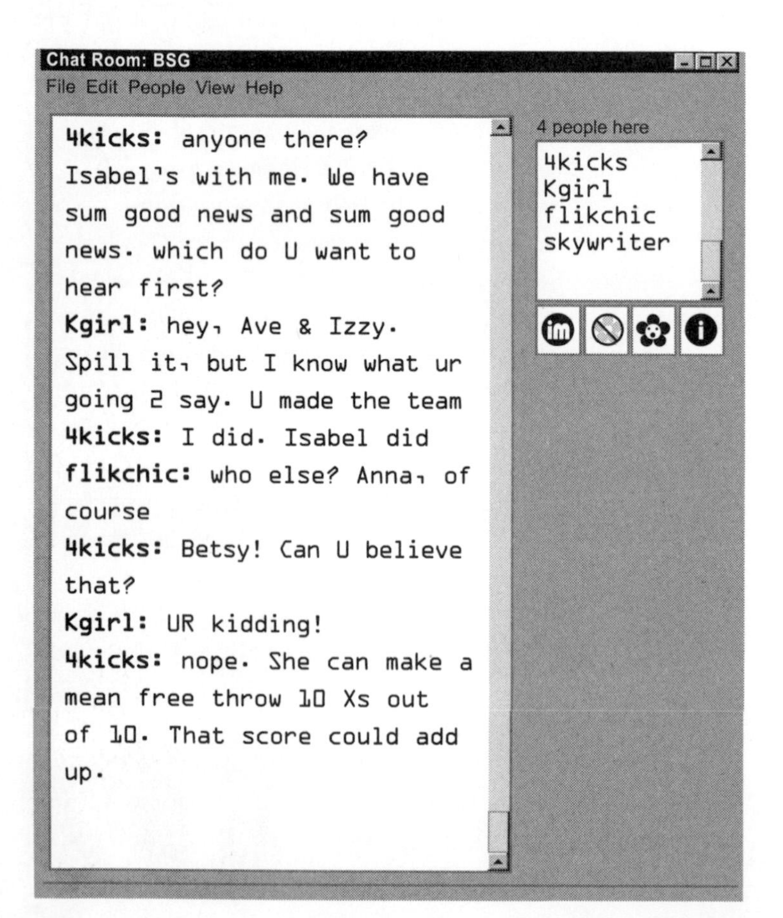

Chat Room: BSG

File Edit People View Help

flikchic: does everything have to B about math?

skywriter: everything is about math

flikchic: OK, OK. Sorry I asked. Tomorrow is D-day

4kicks: Do you think you passed?

flikchic: I hope so

skywriter: wanna walk 2 school 2gether?

4kicks: Deal, Izzy says yes too

flikchic: I'm there

Kgirl: C U then

4 people here

4kicks
Kgirl
flikchic
skywriter

CHAPTER 9

JUMP SHOT!

MAEVE LOOKED sleepy, but she'd gotten up early enough today to walk with the BSG. "Avery, you're going to be the basketball team's star this year. I just know it. Never mind those snooty—and very tall—eighth graders. They won't know what hit them."

"Julie Faber invited Avery to her party yesterday." Isabel dropped this bomb on the group.

"You're kidding!" Maeve danced around a shedding oak tree whose red leaves crunched on the sidewalk and street. "That's great, Avery."

"I'm not going."

"Why not?" Charlotte said.

"I don't think she did it because she wanted to. I think Anna put her up to it."

"Why would she do that?" Charlotte still had trouble believing that Julie Faber would leave Avery out of anything. Avery was always so much fun at a party because she got along with all the boys and managed to get everyone off the sidelines.

"You know Anna and Joline. They just like to cause

trouble. They were hoping I would fall on my knees and say, 'Thank you, thank you, Julie, for inviting me to your great party.' Then they could call me a loser. Forget it. I'm not going."

"I just don't feel right, going without you." Katani shifted her book bag to her other shoulder. "We can still back out if you want us to."

Maeve threw Katani a startled look and frowned. She was torn; she couldn't stand the idea of missing the party, but she didn't want to be disloyal either.

"No way, I'd feel really bad if you didn't go," Ave said.

The girls made their way into the school and through the crowded halls to their lockers. No sooner had they opened them when Kiki Underwood stopped behind Avery.

"I hear you're going to Julie's party after all, Avery."

"Who told you that?" Avery wanted to ignore Kiki, but Kiki was an in-your-face type of person.

"Everyone heard about it. They said Julie felt sorry for you and that she changed her mind."

Charlotte put her hand on Avery's arm, saying, "leave it alone." She hated fighting, even verbal fights, but it looked as if Kiki, Anna, and Joline had decided to stir things up.

All the BSG exchanged looks that said, "Don't take the bait."

"Will your parents still let you go if you flunk the math test, Maeve?" Joline asked.

"Who said I was flunking math?"

"Everyone knows that, too." Joline grinned and looked at Anna for support.

Katani turned to Avery. "Let's change the channel. This soap opera is boooring!"

A lot of seventh graders had gathered around them, hoping for an all-out scene, but Katani charged through the crowd, leading the way to homeroom. The rest of the BSG took her lead.

Once they got into class, Maeve asked, "What was that all about? They seemed determined to pick a fight."

Katani shrugged. "Maybe the zookeepers forgot to come and feed them today."

Maeve giggled and soon all the BSG were laughing.

"What's so funny, girls?" Ms. Rodriguez queried, walking into class and setting her books and purse on her desk. She took off a smashing suede coat, which Katani couldn't take her eyes off, and put it around the back of her chair.

"Oh, we were just conducting tryouts for Abigail Adams' version of *The Three Witches*." Maeve rolled her eyes, and that set her friends off again.

"If you say so." Ms. R smiled. "Better settle down now, however. We have a lot of work to do today."

As third period got closer, Maeve could think of nothing else but math. When the bell rang and she had to make her way down the hall, she practiced the brand new math mantra her father had taught her. He said he learned it from his favorite political science professor in college. She stopped outside the door and took a deep breath. "This grade will not matter in five years. This grade will not matter in five years ..."

"But how can you be so sure, Maeve?" Dillon nudged her across the threshold of the door.

Leave it to Dillon to ruin her meditation exercise. She was just about to drift into class feeling that this test was not going to impact her future success one iota.

The class got quiet in a hurry as soon as Mr. Sherman, dressed in his customary black shirt, black pants, and black sweater, walked to the desk. He had a frown on his face that suggested trouble.

What do you think...
a bad attitude or
just bad hair?
Isabel M.

✿

"Well, I have some good news and some bad news. Which do you want to hear first?"

"The good," Avery said, her confidence high.

"Yes, I agree," Lisa Chen said. "Always get good news first. It helps you accept the bad news."

"Maybe for you, Lisa," Maeve said under her breath. No one heard her except Dillon, who gave Maeve a thumbs-up.

"Most of you passed," Mr. Sherman said. "But on the whole, I was disappointed with the scores. Some of you need to seriously upgrade your study habits." Mr. Sherman was always talking about upgrading things.

Dillon whispered. "He needs to upgrade his tie collection."

Maeve whispered back, "Maybe his teaching skills, too." Through her research, Maeve had learned that a lot of math teachers, brilliant though they be in math, had a hard time teaching difficult-to-teach kids. And she was one of those kids.

"Mr. Johnson and Ms. Kaplan-Taylor ..." [WOW, Maeve was impressed. He actually got her name right this time!] "... Do you have a comment you want to share with the class?"

"No sir." Dillon grinned at Maeve the moment Mr. Sherman turned away.

"The rest of the bad news is that several of you flunked the test. If you happen to be in that minority, please talk to me about the retest."

That could be good news, Maeve thought. Remember the mantra—in five years, this test won't be important. If I make up songs or plays or story problems to help me learn, maybe I'll do better on the retest.

Maeve took her paper from Mr. Sherman, who handed each test out himself so the scores were confidential. Maeve realized that was pretty nice of him. In fact, he had taken time to write a short letter to Maeve, stapling it as the top sheet of her test.

Slowly, she raised the cover sheet until she could see her grade. A big, fat, red F. Her heart pounded and she felt short of breath. No, she was going to stay in control … breathe ... in five years ….

Letting the top sheet fall back into place, she read the letter. Mainly, it said Mr. Sherman would like to follow through on scheduling a conference with Maeve and her parents.

"You OK, Maeve?" Avery whispered from behind her.

Maeve nodded, then turned around a little. "What did you get?"

"I got an A. I studied really hard this time. I want to make good grades."

So do I, Maeve sighed. I studied hard, too. I'd love to make good grades in math. She whispered to herself, "Breathe … in five years ... One F does not a failure make."

Mr. Sherman spent the rest of the period going over the test and asking for questions. Maeve tried to follow along, but the big, fat F was imprinted in her brain. Well, at least she wasn't ready to pass out. That was an improvement. She would have to call her dad and tell him that his mantra had definitely helped.

But, still, when the bell rang, Maeve bolted out of class and down the hall.

Avery and Isabel tried to catch her, but Maeve was hurrying toward the library.

"Poor Maeve," said a sympathetic Katani, who had been waiting outside math C class for her friends. "You know, there has to be a better way to help kids like Maeve learn math. Maeve isn't dumb. She just can't get math the way they teach it in school. I'm going to try to think of some more ways to help her. Will you guys help me?"

✿

"OK," Charlotte said. "I have a book report to rewrite, but I'll make time."

"I will, if I have any spare time after basketball practices." Avery bounced an imaginary basketball all the way to the cafeteria.

"We all will," Isabel promised.

Survival Skills

Maeve entered the library, which at this moment felt like a peaceful island in the South Pacific. She pretended the air was washed clean by ocean breezes. If she tried she could smell salt water, feel the sun, and hear the slap of waves on the beach. She let down her hair, which she'd gathered into a knot before school. Red curls brushed her shoulders as she shook them out.

"May I help you, Maeve?" Ms. Curtis asked. "Is that your math test? How did you—" Ms. Curtis was one of Maeve's favorite teachers. How she seemed to understand that some students needed to approach things in a different way?

"No I didn't. But I have a new plan. I don't want to be a math victim anymore. To start with, which computer can I use? I am going to look up math phobia."

"That's a great idea. Empower yourself to solve problems and you will have a very successful life." Maeve gave the friendly media specialist a grateful smile.

Ms. Curtis had used the exact right words. The sun on the beach got stronger, and Maeve started to feel warm inside and out as Ms. Curtis helped her bring up the first of several sites she could visit.

Practice Time

Avery didn't go out for the basketball team to hang out with Julie Faber and Anna Banana, but since they all made the team, she was going to have to put up with them. The duo was in classic mean mode on Tuesday afternoon at the first team practice.

They were practicing three on one, and Avery was teamed with Anna and Julie on offense, while Amanda was the defender. Anna kept passing the ball to Julie, who passed it back to Anna, who passed it back to Julie. It was like they had some kind of Queens of Mean plan to keep the ball away from her, and Avery was the monkey in the middle, totally left out yet again.

Avery's frustration built until she jumped in, stole the ball from Julie, and charged past the defender for an easy lay-up.

"Avery, that was a nice move," Coach Porter called out, "but in the three on one drill, you need to work together to get by the defender. This is a team sport!"

Anna grinned at Avery. "Show off."

Avery just ignored her. She grabbed the ball and got back in line to run the drill again. This time when she got the ball, she bounce passed to Julie, who passed to Anna, who tossed up an easy shot.

"That's what I like!" Coach Porter cheered. "Teamwork!"

Maybe Avery could learn to work with the Queens of Mean after all. That didn't mean they had to be friends, but Avery was willing to ignore their comments for the sake of the team. Luckily, she got to be partners with Isabel for the next drill.

"They're so ridiculous," Isabel said later as they walked off the court to the locker room. "They were not passing to you on purpose!"

"Yeah, just like she didn't invite me to the party on purpose," said Avery. "But enough about the QOM. How did you like the first practice?"

Isabel smiled. "I had fun! I think I'm going to like being on the team."

"Great!" said Avery. "Hey, did you pass your math test?"

"You know, Ave, I didn't do so great either. C-. I think working with Maeve might help all of us to understand the problems better. My dad said that people have study groups in college all the time."

"Yeah, Tim told me that too. I found when I was refereeing those little kids in soccer, I learned a lot myself."

"I'm going to try to submit a cartoon for the newspaper around that theme."

"You are so cool, Izzy. I could never do a cartoon, not in a zillion years. My drawings are the worst." Isabel started giggling and Avery joined in. Avery's stick figure drawings resembled the artwork outside the kindergarten. The first time Isabel had seen one of them, she had had to squeeze herself from laughing out loud. But, the cool thing was that Avery really didn't care. Isabel had offered to give her a few pointers but Avery said she was happy to let Isabel be the drawing star of the BSG. "I have other things I want to do."

Isabel reminded Avery of her own mother. They both liked to help other people.

In her daydreams Avery thought about being a pro soccer player, but sometimes she wanted to become a lawyer, a judge, or a Supreme Court justice, in that order. Whatever she did, she would help people, too, even if it meant just showing a bunch of kids how to kick a ball. After all, her mom said, "Even a little bit of help can make a difference in someone's life." Avery added, "... in a dog's life, too."

Avery and Isabel laughed while they changed their clothes and walked slowly home, talking about their plans and dreams and hopes for the future. Avery wondered whether the BSG would always stay in contact even when they were in college or out in the world. Would Maeve, for example, call her old friends when she was a famous star?

CHAPTER 10

FIVE YEAR PLAN

NO ONE WAS in the kitchen when Maeve got home from school. Charlotte and her father had given her a ride, so it was early. A note on the kitchen table said that Sam had permission to go home from school with Gary.

She enjoyed the silence of the empty apartment. Usually she was happiest surrounded by people, but this was kind of like a timeout from the world. She hurried to her room and flopped on her bed. Her guinea pigs were resting.

She dug out her new teen magazine to read. She loved reading about the latest fashions and movies. But first, she turned to the horoscope page.

It's time for your stubborn gene to kick in. Don't be like the bull and charge forward, though, or you might find yourself in a china shop. You are smarter than that. Think things through. Take one thing at a time, and be patient, resolve it. Leave time for a romantic interlude. Soon you'll have two lucky days back to back. Enjoy!

Two lucky days paired with a romantic interlude! Maeve leaned back in her chair. Thank goodness. There was nothing about her life turning into a disaster because she flunked her math test.

She opened her notebook.

Notes to Self

1. If Dillon is in eighth grade and I'm in seventh, will he still like me?
2. My parents won't be mad that I flunked my math test, but will they be disappointed? Nobody wants a kid who flunks stuff. Should I act like I don't care that I flunked the test? Maybe they will be impressed when I show them all my research on math phobia.
3. What if they won't let me go to the party? What if they won't let me go anywhere until I study and pass the math test the second time around?
4. What if I'm grounded for the rest of this year?
5. I need a vacation.

Before social studies, Charlotte handed Maeve an envelope full of mail for her "Ask Maeve" column. Now, with the house quiet, was a good time to catch up. She read through the letters and selected one to answer first.

✿

Dear Maeve,

I have a really, really big impossible problem. I'm afraid of my parents. Both of them. Not that they are mean to me or anything. It's just that they always know exactly what I should do anytime a problem comes up. They tell me. And they expect me to do that very thing. If I don't, they yell at me. Don't they know I have a mind of my own? But if I argue, they get mad, and pretty soon I'm grounded. Well, you get the idea.

~ Living in fear

Wow! Maeve thought about what to say. At least when she had a problem, like math, her parents listened to her try to explain it. She was going to sit in on the math conference at school. She didn't know what she'd say, but she'd be there to defend herself.

Dear Fearful,

Your parents may not realize you are not a little kid anymore. Maybe they made a lot of mistakes as a kid and can't stop thinking about that. They think they are doing the right thing. Try writing your parents a letter. Say what you said to me. Let them think it over when you're not there. I'm almost 100% sure they don't want you to be afraid of them. Try talking to them again before you have a problem. Talk about everyday things. That way, it won't seem so hard to approach them about something complicated. I hope this helps. Write me again. I care.

At least Maeve had parents she wasn't afraid of. She leaned back against her big flower pillow and drifted off. As she closed her eyes, a huge red flashing F appeared in her brain. "Be gone" she said out loud, as she waved her hand in the air like a wizard commanding a newt to disappear. *Mmm,* she thought as she drifted off to sleep. *It was wonderful to be in charge.*

PANIC CITY

"Maeve! Are you home? She's home, Ross. Her books are here. Maeve?" Ms. Kaplan climbed up the stairs.

Maeve's door was open. "Here she is, Ross. She's asleep."

Maeve's eyes fluttered. She felt like Sleeping Beauty awakening from a deep 100 year nap.

Ms. Kaplan shook her. "Maeve, wake up. Do you have any idea how worried we were?"

Maeve sat up, rubbed her eyes, and yawned. "Worried? Why? I'm OK."

"Why? I told you I'd pick you up after school and we'd go shopping. I was a few minutes late, but I knew you'd wait for me. When you weren't outside, I waited and waited. Then I went inside, but the school was empty. Mrs. Fields said everyone had gone home."

Maeve blinked her eyes. She forgot a shopping trip? Impossible! See there, the math test and that mind-numbing F had wiped out all her brain cells.

"Mrs. Fields is worried. I need to call her." Maeve's mom popped the cell phone from her pocket, but left the room to dial Ruby Fields' number.

Maeve's father came in the room and sat on her bed. "Maeve, honey, what's wrong? Are you sick?"

Maeve did feel strange, as if she really was Sleeping Beauty, and instead of five or ten minutes, she'd slept for years. "I was just tired. And Dad ..."

"Yes, is there some trouble? Are you in trouble?"

"Sort of. I flunked my math test. I guess that's what made me forget Mom was picking me up. Charlotte offered me a ride and, well ... I'm sorry if I scared you and Mom. What if Mrs. Fields won't let me come back to school?"

"Nonsense. We talked about this. Flunking the test isn't the end of the world."

"Maybe not to you, but I studied and I still flunked it. I just can't understand seventh-grade math."

Mr. Taylor sighed. "I know, Maeve. I understand."

"You do?"

"Yes, now let's go downstairs and talk. We sent Sam back to his friend Gary's house with money to order pizza. We thought we might have to look for you."

"Where would I be?" Maeve said. "What are we having for dinner? I went to the library to look something up, and I missed lunch."

"Well, we can't have you starving, now can we?" Her father reached out and smoothed Maeve's hair like he used to do when she was a sick little girl. "I think we'll go out to some nice quiet little restaurant where we can talk. Would you like that?"

"Yes." Maeve got up. "I have to change clothes. These are all wrinkled."

"Fine. Take your time. I'll make sure our plans are alright with your mother."

Maeve looked in her closet for something colorful, then settled on jeans and a top with multicolored sequins. She washed her face, brushed her teeth, then took a little time with some makeup. Her idea was that if she looked good, she'd feel good.

"Where shall we go?" her dad asked, once they were in the car. "Anna's Taqueria? Do you feel like Mexican?"

"Anna's will be too crowded," Maeve decided. Maybe filled with kids from school. She was worried. Everyone went to Anna's. She didn't want kids to hear her talking about math with her parents. Plus, Maeve hadn't had a moment alone with her parents in a long time. Tonight was special if she could forget why it was happening.

"Someplace quiet," Maeve's mother said, rubbing her forehead. She probably had a headache. Maeve hoped she wasn't the cause of it. It must be hard being a parent, she figured, especially when you had a child who was having trouble in school.

"Sorry, Mom," she said, just loud enough for her mother to hear.

"Someplace near Brookline Village," her mom said. "We can find a restaurant there, and maybe it won't be as crowded."

Once they were settled at a table at the Village Smokehouse, Ms. Kaplan collapsed in her chair, leaning her chin on her elbow, and staring at Maeve's dad. He stared back. Maeve was dying to ask them if they were dating or something. There was a sort of electricity between them that made a part of Maeve wish they could have gone out alone, but then again maybe her math problems were bringing them together again.

The waiter came and her dad ordered coffee, a steak, and a salad.

Her mother said she'd have grilled salmon and a salad.

"Maeve?"

"I'll have a hamburger and lemonade." She studied the menu. "Mom, can I have the mud pie for dessert?"

"Whatever you like," her father said. "This is a celebration. We're celebrating having dinner with our beautiful daughter."

"But dumb."

✿

"You're not dumb, Maeve," Mr. Taylor reassured her. "I want you to banish that word from your vocabulary. There are all kinds of smarts in this world. Don't you think being able to be an actor and make someone laugh or cry with a look or a phrase is a certain kind of genius? You and the rest of the world need to expand your definition of intelligence. So you need some help with your studies. That's no crime. Maybe a different tutor." Both of her parents reached over and patted her hand at the same time.

"No, I like Matt. This isn't his fault. He's patient and nice and he really helps me. Remember how last year I couldn't even manage percentages? Well, I can do them now. My problem is that I have math phobia." When Maeve saw her parents' bemused expressions, she added for emphasis, "I have all the symptoms. Really."

"I don't know, Maeve." Her mother looked skeptical.

"Seriously. Mom. I looked it up. My mind goes completely blank when somebody asks me a question about math. I get nervous when I go to math class. I can't pay attention and my mind wanders, I don't understand when the teacher talks, and I wish I was somewhere else ..."

"Maeve, honey," her mother held up her hand. "I think you make a very good case. But even if you were able to control your anxiety, I think math would still be difficult for you." Her dad nodded in agreement with his wife.

Maeve was really feeling pumped. "I really know that. But listen to this. When my friends helped me study, we made up songs and stories and football cheers to help me remember formulas. I think I can keep doing that and with Matt's help, I can learn how to use those formulas with the right problems. What I can't do is understand what the Crow ..."

"The crow?" both parents looked totally confused.

"I mean Mr. Sherman. I can't understand what he's saying, and he goes too fast, and then I think I am stupid, and it's all over." Maeve's woeful expression caused both parents to laugh.

"It's not funny, you guys," protested Maeve. "I need math therapy."

"Maeve, I'm very proud of you," her mother said after collecting herself. "It sounds as if you've taken some positive steps to help yourself."

"Well, I sort of remembered that my sign is Taurus, and Taurus is a bull, and bulls are stubborn, and I'm going to let my stubborn gene kick in to get over being scared of math."

Her mother and father looked at each other, trying to hold back a smile.

"You can laugh if you like, but I'm your daughter. You probably have some stubborn genes, too."

"No kidding." Her mother laughed and took her dad's hand. They sat there like that, holding hands and looking at a bemused Maeve.

After a nice, slow-paced dinner where they talked about movies and things other than math and Maeve, she went back home full of chocolate mousse and hope.

"May I go up to my room and study?" Maeve asked.

"Yes, but maybe you don't need to study too much tonight. Just go to bed early and start over tomorrow," her mother said, surprising Maeve. Several months ago, she would have said, *Study all night if that's what it takes.*

Maeve got ready for bed but decided to check in with her friends to let them know she was OK. After her nap she wasn't very sleepy anymore.

Chat Room: BSG

File Edit People View Help

flikchic: BSG, lots of news. Mainly I'm not grounded forever

skywriter: I'm so glad

Kgirl: my grandmother said you forgot your mother was picking you up after school to go shopping

4kicks: you forgot to go shopping?

flikchic: unbelievable, isn't it? I came home and fell asleep. My mother was frantic. But, I wasn't missing for long

Kgirl: were they upset over your test?

flikchic: not as much as I thought they'd B. We're working it out. my parents are going 2 help me and I'll get extra tutoring and we are going to talk to Mrs. Fields and Mr. Sherman and stuff. We r going to see if I can take the test over

4kicks: happens 2 every1 sometimes. I'm off. have 2 study ... bye

Chat Room: BSG

File Edit People View Help

3 people here

flikchic
skywriter
Kgirl

Kgirl: I was surprised Avery was on. despite what she says, I think she's bummed about the party.

flikchic: Julie did tell her she could come

Kgirl: yeah, after Anna put her up 2 it 4 a joke

skywriter: would U go if someone invited U as a joke?

flikchic: pause to think. probably

Kgirl: Oh, Maeve, you're hopeless

flikchic: I just like parties. My horoscope said I was going 2 have 2 great days in row, not 2 mention a romantic interlude

skywriter: hey, I'm going 2 read mine

Kgirl: me 2. Bye

Before she went to sleep, Maeve arranged her hair on her pillow to look lovely in case a prince came to discover her in her dreams.

UPSIDE DOWN PLANS

"I can't believe it, Elena," Isabel said. She was almost asleep when Elena came in, shook her, and wanted to talk.

She sat up straight and rubbed her eyes.

"I was foolish, Isabel. I admit it. I was loca. I thought Jimmy Riggs really liked me. He kept begging me to go out. Then when I said I would, when I made all sorts of sacrifices to change my schedule, he decided he'd rather go out with Lilli Harbeck. He just dropped me without even trying to hide what he was doing."

"Papa would say that he was a "*no good hombre.*"

"I don't care. I think the entire school knew what was going to happen way before I did anyway. How could I have been so stupid?" Elena Maria wailed.

"You aren't stupid, Elena. I think that chico was stupid for not wanting to go out with you. Don't waste your time thinking about him." Isabel was outraged that someone would treat her sister like that. Even though Elena could be so annoying, she was her sister.

"You are so nice, Izzy!" Elena started to cry.

"Girls, girls," Aunt Lourdes said, coming into their room.

"What are you fighting about? Why is Elena crying? When I was your age—"

"Elena is crying because I'm too nice," Isabel said, leaving Aunt Lourdes to stare at them both, then turn around and leave.

Elena giggled. "At least she didn't say at her age she was too nice. I'll see you in the a.m." Elena shut the door quietly behind her.

Isabel punched in Avery's number.

"Hey. Isabel, that you? I'm getting ready for bed."

"I was falling asleep reading when Elena woke me up. She was having a major meltdown."

"What happened to Elena?"

"She's just being muy loca. The boy she was going out with just dumped her."

"Nice guy."

"A rat, I think. Anyway, she is going to baby-sit the Fergusons, but I am still going to help her. Those two little devils require a Tag Team approach. You can baby-sit with Elena and me if you want. I don't mind at all."

"Uh, no thanks—I don't really want to hear any more of your sister's tragic romance stories. No offense."

"But what are you going to do on Saturday?"

"I'll find something."

"Yeah. I'm sure something will come up. Well, come over to the Fergusons' if you want. We'll need all the help we can get with those little monsters."

"Maybe."

"I'll pay you half of my share."

"You don't have to do that. I'll talk to you later, Izzy."

"Bye."

☙

Avery shut off her light. What would she do Saturday night? Stay home and stare at Walter shedding his skin? She'd hate to miss that. Suddenly, the tears began rolling down her face and she couldn't stop them. At that moment, her mother opened the door to say goodnight. Avery turned and buried her face into the pillow. Her mother rushed over to her bed and sat down beside her. She put her hands on Avery's head and began to gently stroke her daughter's hair. She didn't say a word. When Avery's sobs finally subsided, her mother simply said, "Tell me about it, sweetheart."

SATURDAY NIGHT SPECIAL
Walter sheds his skin ...
Don't miss it!
To each his own, I guess ...

PART TWO
CRAZY TIMES

CHAPTER 11

READY TO PARTY

WHAT TO WEAR? What to wear? For some reason, Maeve just couldn't think of anything, so she tossed on her favorite sweatshirt from Think Pink and a pair of jeans. She slipped on pink flip flops, thrilled her toenail polish with the pineapples was holding up.

A familiar squeak reminded her she had responsibilities in addition to looking fantastic. She found a mound of dried-up bread crusts and approached her guinea pigs. They leaned on the cage and looked at her, noses sniffing, anticipating something. Anything.

"Today I christen you Salt and Pepper, or should you be Coffee and Cream? Yes, that's better."

Cream jumped on his exercise wheel and did a quick twenty laps before Maeve could get the door open and feed the bread to them.

"Ooh, you are such a little track star. I'm going to sign you up for Abigail Adams cross country." She cooed to her little buddy.

Suddenly, a funny thought came to her. She shared it

aloud to see what Coffee and Cream thought about it.

"If Coffee ran, turning her exercise wheel ten revolutions per minute, and Cream left two days later, turning his exercise wheel fifteen revolutions per minute, which GP would get to eighth grade first?"

Now, which formula should she use to solve the problem? She had no idea. She'd have to ask Matt to help her figure it out sometime.

While Maeve filled the water and pellet bowls, Cream grabbed the biggest crust and took it into an empty toilet paper roll to eat all by himself. He was such a chow hound.

Quickly, she grabbed up all the papers that had fallen off her bed and stuffed them into her backpack along with her books and laptop.

In the kitchen, Sam poured Cheerios into a bowl and drowned them with milk. He kept pushing the tiny brown lifesavers under water to watch them pop back up.

"Eat that cereal, Sam," Ms. Kaplan said. "And, Maeve, please be here right after classes to baby-sit Sam."

Sam grinned at Maeve, jumped up, and froze into a karate chop pose. "And watch out for closet doors."

Maeve's mother looked at her, then her face softened. "Pretty in pink." She hugged Maeve. "But look at your feet. You girls and your flip-flops. Your feet are going to freeze. Eat some breakfast. Since I'm already late, I'll give you a ride as soon as you're ready. You and Sam, too."

Party Buzz

Now that it was almost here, all anyone at Abigail Adams was talking about was Julie Faber's party. Maeve heard the buzz from every small group of girls clumped together around their lockers like schools of bright fish off the beaches of Hawaii.

"What are you wearing? Something Hawaiian or just regular party stuff?" "Hair hanging loose would look better if she gives us leis." "Maybe she'll hand out orchids. You'd need your hair down for that, too."

"Cute headband, Maeve," Katani said when they stopped at their lockers. "What's the occasion?"

"Nothing much, but this sparkly band makes me feel like dancing." Maeve executed a perfect combination, then took one step back to make room for a spin.

"Ooof! Maeve, look before you twirl." Maeve crashed into Dillon, who tried to catch her before she went sprawling onto the floor.

All Maeve could do was laugh at herself. A big splat on the floor in the middle of a busy hallway was too obvious to try and cover up. Maeve figured she better just go with it.

Dillon helped her up from the floor and everyone headed toward the cafeteria.

"Important announcement!" the Yurtmeister shouted as he rushed by. "We're having lasagna for lunch!"

As they entered the cafeteria, Julie Faber, surrounded by her attendants, moved ahead of them. Julie tossed out words like *grass skirts, hula girls, mango-pineapple punch,* and *coconut cake,* loud enough for everyone in a ten mile radius to hear. Lisa Kraft and Yolanda Jones looked over at Avery to gauge her reaction. Avery stared straight ahead. Wise words from her mother rang in her head: "You are better than this silly smallness of spirit." She grabbed a sandwich, strawberry yogurt, and a home-baked chocolate chip cookie. Her mother said she should do everything she wanted this week to make herself happy. And a warm, just-baked chocolate chip cookie looked awfully tasty, Avery thought.

When the Beacon Street Girls found a table as far away as possible from Julie, they sat quietly for a couple of minutes.

"Go ahead, guys, talk about the party," Avery said. "I know you're dying to and I don't care, now."

The tone of Avery's voice was a little mysterious, but it was clear to the BSG that she was going to deal with it in her usual way. Charge ahead. Don't waste time with small petty stuff. Charlotte admired her spunky friend. People could learn a lot from Avery's attitude toward this whole party fiasco. Avery was filled with courage, and Charlotte hoped everyone at Abigail Adams would recognize it some day.

Before anyone could say anything, Chelsea Briggs approached their table. She seemed hesitant to do so, but Charlotte scooted over to make room for her to sit with them.

"Do you mind if I sit down?" Chelsea asked, smiling.

"No problem," Katani said. "How's the photography business doing?"

"It's good, Katani. I printed up those fliers and one of the teachers asked me to take pictures of her daughter's birthday party. But I need an opinion here," Chelsea said as she brushed aside everyone's congratulations. She still wasn't used to people being interested in "the fat girl." Of course, she *had* lost two pounds since she came home from Lake Rescue. Her brother high-fived her this morning when she announced the loss at the breakfast table. "Slow and steady wins the race, dude," he said, but not before giving her a friendly noogie on the head.

"Seriously I really need your opinion about something."

"Shoot," Avery said, jumping up and tossing a make believe basket. "Score three points."

"Julie didn't invite me to her party," Chelsea said, spreading her lunch before her.

"What else is new? I didn't get invited either." Avery looked at Chelsea.

"A BSG didn't get invited?" Chelsea seemed incredulous.

Avery grinned. "Yeah, go figure."

"It's really an outrage," chimed in Katani.

"Go ahead, Chelsea," encouraged Charlotte.

"Well, then she came to me this morning and asked me to take pictures. It seems the high-priced photographer they had hired backed out on them. He probably got a better job. They can't get anyone else, so they asked me. I guess I'm good enough to take photos, but not to be a guest. My mother said it was my choice. But the whole thing is so weird I don't know what to do. I thought I would ask you all … I mean, what do you think?"

At first there was silence around the table. No one could believe how tacky Julie Faber and this whole *who is invited, who is not* had become.

Finally, Katani shrugged. "No big deal, Chelsea. Consider it a job. There are times when you have to separate business from pleasure."

Isabel clapped and then all the BSG laughed. When it came to business, Katani was all business.

"Charge them big bucks," Maeve suggested. "Ask what they were paying the unreliable professional and get at least half that."

"Why not charge what the original photographer was getting?" Isabel asked.

"Oh, I can't do that yet. I'm not a professional—someday, but not now." Chelsea stirred her cottage cheese.

"But they're in a pinch, aren't they?" Avery offered Chelsea some almonds. "They need you. That's when professionals raise their rates."

"I don't know ... is that right?" Chelsea looked up from her cottage cheese.

"Chelsea has to keep her integrity." Charlotte took a bite of the spicy lasagna. "Or people won't trust her business?"

"So you think I should take the job?" Chelsea said spooning some fruit and cottage cheese onto some crackers.

"Of course. Each job leads to the next." Katani smiled. "As soon as I started putting a Kgirl label on the little clutch bags I designed, people came to me and asked to buy my stuff. People love original designs."

"I know. Everybody was talking about your bags in photo class. Maddie Westheimer was showing off her black and pink one. It was so cool."

Katani blushed but was pleased with the compliment.

"Get a stamp with your name and logo to put on the packages of finished photos you deliver," Isabel said. "I'll help you design a logo."

"Thanks. You guys are great. You should start a company called BSG Inc." Chelsea grabbed a carrot. "Oops, I gotta go." Chelsea jumped up from the table. "I'm meeting with Mr. Sherman. Do you believe how hard that math test was? I almost flunked it."

Maeve blinked. Chelsea had had done poorly too. She felt bad for Chelsea, but also comforted that somebody she knew was having trouble as well. She didn't feel so alone. She wondered just how many people flunked the test. She was going to ask around. Maybe they could get Mrs. Fields to start a special after-school group. They could call it "Math Victims No More."

The lunch bunch broke up. Avery was glad Chelsea had come along to distract them from party talk, or to bring a different kind of party talk.

✿

But they weren't home free yet. Before the BSG could leave the cafeteria, Anna and Joline crept up behind them. "So what, is Chelsea Briggs going to be in your little club now?" Joline asked.

"Something wrong with having good friends, Joline?" Maeve asked.

"As long as they don't act like boring old movie stars," Anna said.

"And can count to ten," added Joline, giving Maeve a snide look.

Before any of the BSG could think of a comeback, Anna laughed and they both rushed down the opposite hall.

"Wow, I really do look like Rita Hayworth," Maeve said. "Even those two recognized the incredible resemblance." She tossed her hair over her shoulder and twirled around.

"Do you think late at night, when they think about what they've done, they ever feel guilty?" asked Isabel.

Katani, Maeve, Charlotte, and Avery looked at each other. After a pause they yelled in unison "NOOO!"

Charlotte glanced at Maeve, glad she was in a good mood after yesterday's disaster. "Are we all getting together this afternoon?"

"Isabel and I have basketball practice," Avery said.

"And I'm helping my mother with her exercises after practice," Isabel said proudly. "Her physical therapist taught me how. So I'll probably talk to you guys tomorrow then."

"Oh, that's so cool Isabel," said Maeve. "How is your mom doing?"

"She's good, thanks for asking Maeve," answered Isabel.

"Can I take Marty for a walk after practice, Charlotte?" asked Avery.

"Sure, we'll be home all night. I have a ton of homework

and my dad wants me home for dinner," Charlotte said as she turned in her lunch tray and the BSG walked out of the cafeteria and into the crowded hallway. "He wants to talk about winter vacation plans."

"Are you going away for vacation?" asked Katani, just as the bell rang signaling the end of lunch period.

"Come on, Charlotte," interrupted Avery, "let's hurry! We don't want to be late for science!"

Avery grabbed Charlotte's arm and started booking it for the science lab. Charlotte waved good-bye to Katani, Isabel, and Maeve and tried not to trip as Avery dragged her along.

"Whoa, slow down Ave!" Charlotte exclaimed.

"We're using the microscopes today, Charlotte!" Avery said as they turned the corner toward the math and science wing, narrowly avoiding colliding with a group of loitering eighth grade girls. "I've been looking forward to this class all week!"

Avery and Charlotte arrived at the science lab with plenty of time to spare and managed to snag their favorite lab bench by the windows on the far side of the lab. Each bench had two lab stations, a small sink, and four high stools. Today there was a microscope, pipette, and slides at each station. The girls looked around the classroom, and noticed eight jars of what looked like dirty water on the teacher's work bench at the front of the classroom. At the chalkboard, Mr. Moore, the science teacher, was putting the final touches on a drawing of a cell labeled "Amoeba."

Nick Montoya and Henry Yurt entered the room shortly after the girls, and sat down at the other station at their bench.

"Hi, Charlotte," said Nick. "How's it going, Ave?"

Charlotte gave a little wave and smiled, and Avery launched into about how psyched she was to do lab experiments. Charlotte was happy too, because science was one of her favorite subjects; she just wasn't as vocal about it as Avery was.

"And I also can't wait to get to the unit on ecology," continued Avery.

"I just hope this experiment doesn't have anything to do with sulfur," Yurt said. "We could all go home smelling like rotten eggs."

"Ew, yeah, that would be gross," said Avery, scrunching up her nose.

The bell rang signaling the start of class and the science teacher, Mr. Moore, called for everyone to sit down.

"Alright class," said Mr. Moore from his work station at the front of the lab, "last week we started our unit on cells. Today we're going to be looking at some single-cell organisms from right here in Brookline. Please take out your lab books and turn to page 45."

Avery reached in to her backpack and pulled out her book and opened it. At the top of the page in large letters it said: Protozoans.

"Protozoans are single-celled organisms," Mr. Moore explained, as he gestured toward the jars of cloudy water. "For this activity, you'll work with your lab partner, using your microscopes to identify the protozoans that are found in these pond samples that I collected from Hall's Pond."

"Cool," Nick said out loud. He loved knowing how everything worked.

"First we'll go over the materials and instructions," Mr. Moore explained, and then he proceeded to read the instructions from the lab book to the class. When he was finished, he said, "And be sure to draw all the microorganisms that you observe in your lab books. OK, one partner from each group may now come to the front and get a sample of pond water."

Avery jumped down from her stool and was the first student to reach the front of the classroom. She grabbed a jar of pond water and returned to the lab bench, followed closely by the Yurtmeister.

"Mmm, smells great," Henry Yurt said as he took a whiff of his jar of pond water. "Our sample has lots of algae in it. That must be what the protagonists eat!"

"It's protozoans, not protagonists, Yurt," Nick corrected with a laugh.

"Well, I suppose a protozoan could be a protagonist," added Charlotte. "Harry Amoeba and the Goblet of Fire." The kids liked the idea of an amoeba as the main character of a story.

Suddenly, Mr. Moore appeared by their lab bench. "While I'm glad that you find single-cell organisms so amusing, I'd like to remind you that you only have 30 more minutes to finish this activity."

"Certainly, Mr. Moore," said Henry in his best official president voice. "Back to work, classmates!"

Mr. Moore chuckled as he moved on to the next table.

"OK," said Charlotte, "first we have to collect the sample."

"Alright, I got that," Avery said, as she picked up a pipette. "Mr. Moore said the best sample would be found at the bottom of the jar."

Avery used the pipette to collect a tiny amount of water and place a few droplets on the microscope slide. Then Charlotte placed the cover slip over the sample and placed it under the microscope.

"Do you want to look first, Avery?" asked Charlotte.

"Sure!" Avery answered, and she looked into the

microscope and focused it by turning the knob on the side of the microscope. "Whoa! There's tons of stuff moving around in there! Oh, there's Harry! Take a look, Charlotte."

Charlotte looked into the microscope and was surprised to see a little world of busy little organisms. She laughed when she realized what Avery was referring to. In the middle of the view was a blob-shape that was moving across the slide that looked just like the amoeba that Mr. Moore had drawn on the board. It was Harry Amoeba! She could see the nucleus of the amoeba and other organelles inside the cell wall.

"Let's start making our drawings of the amoeba," Charlotte said, pulling out her color pencils.

Avery took another look through the microscope when Charlotte started her sketch. "Whoa! I think Harry just ate something! The blob just engulfed some other little microscopic thing!"

The whole class was engrossed in observing the tiny little organisms in the pond water. Avery thought it was amazing that she had never even heard of amoebas or paramecium, and they were swimming around in Hall's Pond all this time.

"Charlotte, I just thought of something. Once I went swimming in Walden Pond—does that mean I was swimming with protozoans?" Avery wondered.

"Sure, there are microorganisms everywhere, Avery," answered Charlotte.

"That kind of gives me the creeps," said Avery.

"Just think of them as protagonists instead of protozoans, Avery," joked Charlotte. "They're just little heroes trying to live out their story in the pond!"

"Alright class, time to clean up," announced Mr. Moore. "I hope everyone observed a variety of protozoans in their sample. Be sure to label the microorganisms you drew."

Charlotte returned the jar of pond water to Mr. Moore's desk, and Avery cleaned off their microscope slide in the sink, and the pond water was washed off down the drain.

"Good-bye, Harry!" Avery said with a forlorn expression on her face. Avery loved animals so much, she was even sad to say good-bye to a protozoan!

Queens of the Basketball Court

Even though she was feeling down, Avery tried to stick with her mom's advice—do things that make you happy. For Avery, that meant putting all her energy into one of her favorite things ... basketball. When she was on the court, concentrating on making the next shot or playing defense, Avery forgot all her troubles. That is, until Julie Faber or her friends made a snide comment and she was reminded of the party all over again.

"Hey Betsy, try to pass it to me next time instead of the red team," Julie said as she ran by her. The team had spilt into two teams for a full court scrimmage, and unfortunately Coach Porter had put Isabel on the red team and Avery on the blue team with both Julie and Betsy.

"Give her a break, Julie," Avery said, frowning. "Amanda made a nice play to steal that pass!"

"Focus on the game, Avery," Coach Porter called from the sideline.

That was one of the most annoying things about Julie—she never got caught by the teachers when she was picking on people. This time, Avery was only trying to stick up for her teammate, and she was the one who got in trouble!

Avery forced her attention back to the scrimmage and to guarding her player. Amanda Cruz passed the ball to Isabel, who dribbled a few steps away from her defender, Betsy, before passing it to a wide open Jenny Pesky under the basket.

Where is Julie? thought Avery as she watched Jenny bounce an easy shot off the backboard and straight through the hoop. Julie should have been guarding Jenny.

Coach blew the whistle. "Alright girls, that's enough for today. Red team wins 15-14. Everybody run a cool-down lap and stretch."

Maybe if Julie hadn't been so busy teasing Betsy, she would have been paying attention to guarding her player, and the blue team would have won. Mean players were totally bad for team morale, and Avery was beginning to think their team had enough of them to seriously hurt Abigail Adams' chances for a good season.

After stretching, Avery and Isabel walked into the locker room, and Betsy Fitzgerald hurried to catch up with them.

"Thanks for sticking up for me," Betsy said earnestly to Avery. "I really didn't mean to throw the ball away like that"

"It's no problem, Betsy," said Avery as she changed into her street clothes.

"And thanks for all the tips," Betsy continued in a rush. Sometimes Betsy didn't seem to stop to breathe when she talked. "Are you busy tomorrow? Do you want to come over to my house and practice? I could use some help with the defensive plays."

"Uh ... I don't know," Avery glanced at Isabel, hoping she could help her out with an excuse. Working with Betsy at practice was one thing, but Avery didn't want to hang out with her on the weekend. She stuffed her gym clothes into her bag.

"Didn't you say your mother had something planned for tomorrow?" asked Isabel.

"Oh, right, that thing my brother and I have to do." Avery felt a little guilty avoiding Betsy like that, but she really didn't want to spend her Saturday listening to the perfectionist seventh grader that drove them all crazy talking about college 24/7.

"Oh, OK," Betsy said, looking disappointed. "Well, if it turns out you're free, give me a call."

"Er, right. See you later Betsy." Avery hurried out of the locker room, Isabel following close behind.

"Ave?" Isabel said just before they were ready to split. "Are you really OK about not going to Julie Faber's party?"

Avery took a deep breath. "This whole thing about me being immature really bugs me. Just because I don't like the same things that Anna and Joline like doesn't mean I'm immature. I don't understand why Julie skipped me and invited all the rest of the BSG. She had to know that would make me feel bad. And I can't understand why someone would want to do that to someone who has never done anything mean to them."

"Maybe she never even thought about it. Do you think she snubbed you intentionally?"

"It was a pretty obvious snub. I think Anna and Joline put her up to it."

"Probably. She even invited me, and I'm new to the school. You've probably known Julie forever."

"Listen, Isabel, the last thing I want is for anyone else to know that I'm bummed out about it ... you know, it's embarrassing ... but no biggie. I'm over it. I just want it to be next Monday. Promise me you won't tell the rest of the BSG I said anything."

"I promise, Avery. I feel so bad that we're not going to hang out tomorrow. Can you find something else fun to do?"

✿

"Something more fun than baby-sitting?" Avery laughed. "I think I can do that. Hey, if I'm desperate, I can go coach Betsy on her basketball game and make a few dollars." Avery laughed and gave Isabel a high five. "See you Monday."

Avery ran the rest of the way home, the wind whipping across her face. She felt like shouting out loud. It was such a great feeling, better maybe than Julie fabulous Faber's party!

CHAPTER 12

ଋ

TO PARTY OR NOT?

DESPITE PROMISING herself that she wouldn't think about the "party of the year" anymore, Avery got up Saturday morning feeling kind of sad. She hadn't felt so bad since all the fighting during the student elections when she and Katani were competing against each other. "Why me?" she said aloud. "Why did she have to pick on me?"

"What would you do, Walter?" she asked her pet snake. Walter was not all that responsive. Snakes weren't really that interested in their owners. And he surely wouldn't have an answer to her problem, but he was good to talk to anyway. You can't get really embarrassed in front of a snake. Lifting him out of his aquarium, Avery let him wrap around her hand and test the air with his tiny black tongue. He really was a beautiful snake.

"You have any ideas, Frogster?" she said, after she put Walter back. Frogster looked at her with a cute froggy expression, but didn't have any suggestions either.

"Who are you talking to, Avery?" Her mother asked as she walked into the room and looked around.

"Walter and Frogster." Avery started making her bed and her mother got on the opposite side to help.

"Is your mind still on the party? Thinking everyone else is going except you?"

Her mother was a mind reader. After their first talk Avery had hardly mentioned the party. She just hadn't wanted to think about it.

After working so hard to be a tough, nothing-bothers-me type of person, Avery wiped a tear from her eye.

"Oh, Avery." Her mother gave her daughter a hug. "Everyone gets left out sometimes, but it's never fun."

"I don't see Maeve or Katani ever being left out. Or Anna or Joline, for that matter. And anyway, why would Julie do such a thing, Mom? I've tried and tried to understand, but it just doesn't make sense. I never did anything to her!"

Her mother pulled her down to sit on the bed. She took a deep breath. "You know, Avery, I'll bet she really doesn't know either. But it just may have something to do with power. Often, when you reject or exclude someone, it makes you feel superior. It's not true, but somebody immature might think it's true."

"The BSG think that Anna and Joline put her up to it. Anna was whispering to people and laughing at me at basketball tryouts."

Mrs. Madden heard the names Anna and Joline enough times that Avery didn't have to explain who they were. "Maybe Julie wants those two girls to be her friends. She may have thought this was a way to make that happen."

"Then Julie is going to get hurt, too. As soon as the party is over, Anna and Joline will return to their tight twosome."

"Do you think causing trouble is the only way Anna and Joline have of getting attention? If that's true, that's really sad."

"Anna put Julie up to inviting me to the party at the last minute." Avery picked at a thread on her bedspread. She sniffed a couple of times, then got a tissue and blew her nose.

"Do you want to go under those circumstances?"

"And have everyone at the party laughing at me? No way. I get so angry just thinking about it. I'm left with nothing to do except visit with Walter and Frogster."

"Which can't be terribly stimulating." Her mother smiled and hugged Avery again. "Maybe we can think of something to do together tonight. Would you be open to that?"

"I guess."

Mrs. Madden kept her arm around Avery and walked her down to the kitchen to make breakfast.

"What's up, Ave?" Scott, her 16-year-old brother, asked. He was already frying bacon and getting out eggs for his weekend breakfast special.

Scott really liked to cook. He was getting pretty good at it, too, especially with breakfast.

"Want to do something today? Go lift weights? Shoot some hoops?" Scott cracked six eggs into a bowl and added a splash of milk, then shredded cheese.

"Maybe." Avery took a slice of toast and smeared it with raspberry jam.

"I have a great idea for both of you," their mother said.

Avery looked at Scott. *Not my fault*, her look said.

"There's a charity event at Children's Hospital tonight. I could sure use some help."

"Can those kids you work with play basketball, Mom?" Avery asked. "I don't mind helping them with shooting hoops. That would be fun."

"Not those kinds of games, honey, Poker, a 21-table—"

"Gambling? You're gambling, Mom?" Scott looked at

✿

Avery and made an ultra surprised face.

"OK, OK, you two. Las Vegas nights are often a great way to make money for an organization, and people feel OK about gambling because it's for a good cause. It's perfectly legal, so don't worry about my being arrested. No one keeps the money they win. All the proceeds go to the hospital, most of it goes to the kids' cancer ward."

"So you want us to come over and play poker?" Avery kept a straight face. She loved giving her mother a bad time. She took everything so seriously.

Mom sighed and snatched a bite of the shredded cheese. She tried to look stern, but was losing the battle. "I need your help ..."

"Like teaching them to play poker. Sounds fun, Mom." Scott grinned. "*Ocean's 11*. Count me in."

Mrs. Madden stared at both of them for a few seconds. Then she shook her head and grinned. "Alright you two smart-alecks. I want you to come with me this morning to help set up and visit with the kids. Then we'll come home, change into nicer clothes, and then it's party time ... for a good cause."

Avery couldn't believe it. Wait a minute. Working at the hospital all day and all night wasn't exactly what she wanted to do. In an instant, she had gone from having no plans to having a really busy day, with not even a moment to breathe, or more importantly, walk Marty. But she guessed it would take her mind off Julie's party, and all of the pre-party plans at Charlotte's house. And it would keep her from feeling sorry for herself. It sure beat snake and frog sitting.

Maeve, Katani, and Charlotte would be calling back and forth all day long checking to see what everyone was wearing. In fact, they'd probably go over to Charlotte's to get dressed. Katani would apply everyone's makeup. Then she would add finishing touches to clothing choices, making sure they all looked just a little unique and in style. Avery didn't want to be thinking about all her friends together. They invited her to come over but Avery thought that would be totally horrible. She would feel like a complete loser.

"We're trapped," Scott said to Avery when their mother went to get dressed.

"Yeah, but Scott, think about it. We don't spend much time with Mom anymore. Don't you think she gets lonely?"

"I think she keeps too busy to think about being lonely. But sure, she probably would like a date occasionally. Wouldn't we all?"

Avery groaned. "Speak for yourself, Scotty." Avery ducked and laughed when Scott threw a paper towel at her. "These eggs are awesome, Scott."

Her brother beamed.

"You know Ave, I might have my own restaurant when I grow up."

"Cool," Avery enthused in between mouthfuls of eggs. "Can I work there?"

"Definitely dude."

"What kind of restaurant would you have?" Avery asked.

Scott's face lit up. "I'm going to serve Asian food and hamburgers and hot dogs. I could call it Korea Joe's. What do you think?"

Avery's eyes widened. "Cooool!" Her heart thumped. Scott was the best brother ever.

"So Ave, how's basketball going?"

"Great. We have our first game coming up."

"Who made the team?" Scott asked.

"Well a lot of eighth graders, plus me and Isabel, Anna

McMasters, Julie Faber, and you'll never guess who else."

"Who?" asked Scott.

"Betsy Fitzgerald!" said Avery as she took a bite of eggs. "She's this crazy overachiever at school who studies like six hours a night, and also practices free throws ten hours a day."

"Practice makes perfect, kiddo, especially in sports."

"That's what Betsy said!" Avery continued to munch on her breakfast.

At that moment, Avery's mother came back in the kitchen ready to go. "Five minutes, kids."

Mrs. Madden poured herself one more cup of coffee and sat at the table to make some lists.

A light bulb clicked on in Avery's head. "Mom, I just had a great idea. If Isabel can come, could we circle by and pick her up? Just for the day? She's baby-sitting tonight."

"Absolutely. We need all the help we can get with the kids."

Avery picked up the phone and punched in Isabel's number. "Izzy, what are you up to today?"

"Nothing, really. Just sketching in my note book. You have any ideas?"

"I do. Well, my mom does." Avery explained her plan, Isabel agreed, and said she could be ready ASAP.

Avery gathered some things in a tote bag that might come in handy for entertaining kids. She put her basketball in the car, just in case. Suddenly, a smirk came over her face as she wondered how much chaos a loose basketball could cause at a Hawaiian party.

Aunt Lourdes' apartment was right on their way to the hospital. Mrs. Madden stopped and honked.

"Hi, Mrs. Madden, Scott," Isabel said when she ran out and got in the car. "Thanks for letting me come."

"We need help for the event at the hospital, Isabel," Mrs. Madden said. "It's great you could join us."

"What's happening at home?" Avery asked.

"Oh, Elena is still mad about her boyfriend. I mean her ex-boyfriend. Mama is feeling kind of tired today, and Aunt Lourdes kept thinking of things for us to clean to keep us busy. The usual."

"Is your mother any better, Isabel?" Mrs. Madden asked.

"She is, but her energy goes up and down. Multiple sclerosis does that a lot. My dad is visiting next week for a whole week, though, and that will make us all feel good."

This Is Work?

Boston was a straight shot from Brookline and they had good luck with the traffic. They got to the big hospital complex quickly. Children's Hospital of Boston was world famous, and when Avery first came to America, she was treated for dehydration there. Ever since, Mrs. Madden had been committed to working on fundraisers for them. She believed in giving back to her community, especially one that had helped her baby girl.

As they neared the cancer wing, Avery started to feel queasy. What if the cancer ward was depressing? Seeing bed after bed of kids who had lost all their hair was making her nervous. She took Isabel's hand and squeezed it.

Isabel squeezed back. "Hospitals can be a little scary sometimes," she whispered.

Avery, Isabel, and Scott stood at the door as if that was as far as they could go. "What should we do, Mom?" Avery finally said.

Mrs. Madden motioned for a woman in a clown suit to come meet them. Avery took a deep breath. She had always

✿

been a little bit frightened of clowns. When she was little, she thought the white paint was their real face. She even asked a clown once if he slept in the makeup.

"Marilyn, these are two of my children. Scott is 16 and Avery is 12. And this is Avery's friend, Isabel. They're all yours for as long as you need them." After introductions, their mother turned and left. They were stuck.

"Let's see. Unless you'd like to be a clown, I guess I'll assign Scott the book and game cart. Isabel and Avery, what about snacks? These kids get up at 7 a.m. for meds, so they're ready for a snack now. If someone needs a partner, Scott, maybe you can play games with some of them in turn. You'll find things to do, don't worry. The kids will help you. They'll ask for what they want or need. They are really regular kids and just want to have fun too."

Marilyn, the clown, disappeared. Relieved to say good-bye, Avery and Scott looked at each other and walked into the ward. Isabel followed Avery.

"Look, Izzy, there's a dog playing with that kid. I didn't know they allowed dogs in hospitals. This is so cool." A small boy was rolling a ball. A Golden Retriever ran after the ball, brought it back, and the boy rolled it again.

One of the nurses explained that the dog was a special pet therapy dog trained to work with sick children.

"Hi, Avery," a voice got their attention away from the dog. "I didn't know you volunteered here. Is that boy getting out the game cart your brother? He's really cute. Hi, Isabel."

The voice came from Betsy Fitzgerald. She seemed to be *everywhere* Avery went lately. Surprise Basketball Star-Shooter. Super Hospital Volunteer. The badge Betsy wore was hanging with bars that marked how long she'd worked and the many hospital awards she'd received.

"How do you have the time to work here, Betsy?" Avery asked. "Seems like you study every minute of every day."

"No, you just have to be well organized. You know me. I have a calendar where I lay out my week, my month, and some dates farther ahead. I plan my study time, and now I have to put all the basketball practices and games on it. I might have to give up sewing quilts for seniors in the nursing homes, though. And I never have time for parties." Betsy's face flushed a bit at that last comment. No one wanted to be left out of Julie's party. Avery and Izzy knew that she was just covering up that she wasn't invited either.

Without looking at each other, the threesome shared an awkward moment of silence about the party.

"Yeah, you might have to give up something." She nodded her head toward Scott. "That's my big brother, Scott. He wants to open his own restaurant, you know. We both got kind of trapped today by saying we didn't have anything to do. My mother volunteers here."

"Some people think it's really depressing to work here, but I don't. The kids are nice. I really like them. They are very brave, you know. Come and meet Charlie."

Betsy pulled Avery and Isabel over to a bed where a pretty young girl with the bluest eyes Avery had ever seen smiled a huge smile.

"Hi, I'm Charlie. My real name is Charlotte, but everyone calls me Charlie."

"I'm Avery, and this is Isabel," Avery introduced. "We have a best friend named Charlotte, too."

"Are you going to work here? I hope so. I'll bet you're good at sports, aren't you, Avery?"

"What gave it away? My warmup suit or my basketball shoes?" Avery grinned back.

"I wanted to play basketball," Charlie said. "Now I'm not so sure. I'm in remission. That means that I don't have cancer right now, but I still have a couple more treatments. I'd give a quarter just to go outside for a little while. My mother's here today. If I get permission, can you take me outside?"

Betsy looked at Avery and Isabel, who both shrugged. They didn't know any of the rules. "I'm sure that's OK if your mother and Marilyn agree," Betsy said.

"I saw a park across the street," Avery said. "I wish we had Marty with us. He'd love to play with the kids. There's a basketball hoop too. I always leave my basketball in the car."

"Will your brother help us if some other kids want to go?" Betsy looked around. "Chris could go. He's in remission, too, and feeling pretty good. I think Jadie's mother is here today. She could get permission. I think everyone is at the end of their treatment program, that's why the dogs can come in. We'll just have to get passes for the kids to go."

Just then, Marilyn showed up, and Avery hoped she wasn't going to spoil the field trip for the kids. Charlie was beaming ear to ear and jumping up and down. "Please don't say no, Marilyn, please."

"They have to go in wheelchairs," Marilyn said after hearing their plan. "And one volunteer per wheelchair. That's four kids."

A fourth kid that everyone called Louie-Louie ran up saying he could go. His mother had said yes. Avery was glad they'd brought Isabel. She didn't want to disappoint any of these kids.

"And, Charlie," Marilyn said, "I think you'd better have an adult along. Do you think your mother would go?"

"My mom's game for anything," Charlie said. "She's so much fun. She's helping Bonita, but let me ask her."

A half hour later, the small party of kids wearing hats and riding in wheelchairs, along with their volunteers, arrived laughing at the park. Both Charlie's mother and Jadie's mother agreed to go. They strolled along behind the bustle of kids, probably glad to be outside in the warm fall sunshine, too.

"I feel as if I've escaped," Charlie said. "Will you help me throw that ball, Avery?"

Avery looked at Charlie's mother. She nodded that the game was OK. "For just a little while, Charlie," she said. "You know you always forget how quickly you get tired."

They had played ball in the park for about a half hour, when Chris said, "Hey, lunch. We forgot about lunch. I'm getting hungry."

Chris's white teeth stood out against his walnut-colored face. He grinned all the time, but right now looked dismayed. It was the first time in weeks that he had been hungry, and he wanted some good food now!

"I'm so tired of hospital food," Jadie said. "I wish we could have a pizza. Or hamburgers."

"Hamburgers! Yeah, hamburgers!" All the kids shouted over and over until everyone was laughing.

"Yea!" Charlie smiled brightly. "Have you got some money, Mom?"

Both Charlie's mother and Jadie's mother nodded and agreed to having lunch outside the hospital. "We're tired of hospital food, too," Jadie's mother laughed.

"No one told us what time to come back." Scott looked at Avery.

"There's a burger place up on the corner." Avery didn't usually eat fast food, but she was willing to give these kids whatever they wanted. And to make their time out of the hospital special.

✿

"I've got money, too." Jadie waved a 10-dollar bill she pulled from the small purse in her wheelchair.

"Me too." Chris pulled some bills from his pockets.

"I have some money, too," piped in Miss Prepared-for-Anything Betsy Fitzgerald.

"I guess that's not a problem then." Avery smiled. "Let's go."

Scott pushed Louie's wheelchair. Louie started singing, "Heigh-ho, heigh-ho, it's off for food we go." Avery chuckled, realizing that they were having their own party, right there, right then. Her mother was right ... the kids at the hospital were just like any other kids. She pushed Charlie's chair. Isabel took Jadie and Betsy walked with Chris. The two mothers stayed close but didn't interfere with the kids' fun. In fact, they seemed to be enjoying the field trip, too.

"Let's not go inside," Jadie suggested when they reached Burger Stop. "We can read the menu and go through the drive-up window. After all, we're sort of driving up. It will be fun ... and unique."

"Good idea. Then we can eat out here at that purple table." Charlie laughed.

The mothers decided to sit down at the table and wait for the kids.

Avery and crew made sure there were no cars coming, pushed the chairs up to the speaker, ordered, then rolled on up to the takeout window.

A girl with an important expression leaned out the window. "Hey, you can't go through the drive-thru window."

"Why not?" Avery asked.

"You have to have a car to do that. You'll have to come inside to order your food."

Four faces lost their party look. "That's no fun," Chris said.

"That's the rule." The girl at the window was adamant.

"Is your boss here?" Scott asked.

"No, I'm the boss right now. Only cars can come through the drive-up window. That's the rule, and I can't let you start breaking rules. There's a reason to have rules." The girl was off with a huge lecture. It sounded to Avery like she was in love with having the power to make people do what she wanted.

"Doesn't she understand there's a time to break rules?" Isabel whispered. "... Especially when it doesn't hurt anyone and is no big deal."

"Never mind," Scott said. "We'll eat someplace else."

"But I wanted to eat here. Burger Stop is my favorite and I haven't had one in so long." Chris looked especially sad.

"I hate rigid rules," Isabel said. "I have an idea. Are you all game?"

"Sure," Charlie said. "We're tired of rules. Let's break some rules."

"We're not going to break any rules. But it will be a little while before we eat. Everyone good to go? OK?" Isabel turned Jadie's chair back toward the sidewalk. "Follow me, team."

Avery and Scott looked at each other. Neither had any idea what Isabel was up to. Avery just shrugged her shoulders. One thing she knew for sure was that Isabel was up to something very creative.

"OK!" a chorus of voices shouted.

"OK!" Isabel echoed.

CHAPTER 13

MORE WAYS THAN ONE

BACK ON THE STREET, they all turned to Isabel. "What's your plan?" Louie asked, his face bright with eager enthusiasm. Isabel took a deep breath. She didn't want to fail their new friends, who had been cooped up for so long. She crossed her fingers and began to outline her idea, hoping it was a good one.

"You remember that furniture store we passed to get here?"

"Yeah, the one on the corner." Avery didn't know what furniture had to do with lunch. She hoped Isabel knew what she was doing.

"Well, furniture stores always have big boxes out back. Surely this one isn't any different." Isabel grinned.

Scott grinned and caught on immediately. "A car ... we're going to make a car. Great idea, Isabel." One of the mothers clapped her hands. "This is delightful."

"The only problem is that I wish I'd brought my paints, and I nearly always carry a sketch book, but I was in a hurry this morning."

Betsy pointed across the busy street. "While you're in the furniture store, I'll go over to that drugstore. What do you need? A little bit of paint and some pens won't cost much."

"Good thinking, Betsy," said Avery giving her thumbs up.

"We can't take too long, so we'll need scissors—a couple pairs of good, sharp ones—and magic markers, all colors. We won't take the time to paint." Isabel thought for a moment. "That should do it."

Scott, Avery, Isabel, and Betsy emptied pockets and purses. They dumped their money onto the sidewalk, counted all their pennies, dimes, and nickels. Chris contributed a few bills, but all of them needed to save enough for lunch.

"This should be more than enough." Betsy scooped up the money and headed for the crosswalk. "I'll meet you at the furniture store if you can help push Jadie."

The wheelchairs paraded up the sidewalk and into the furniture store. Avery suggested they do that so if they met another rules Scrooge at the store, he'd realize they really needed a box. "We might as well use these wheelchairs to our advantage," laughed Jadie.

"Well, well, what do we have here?" a young salesman said with a happy smile. "To what do I owe the honor of this visit?" He probably guessed they didn't want to buy furniture or a new refrigerator.

"We need a box," Charlie said, smiling back.

"A big box," Chris added.

"Well, we do have boxes," the man, whose name tag read Mr. Kelly, nodded his head. "What size big box do you need?"

"Refrigerator, I guess," Isabel said, measuring three wheel chair lengths with her hands. "I think one person will have to double up unless they make really tall fridges these days. But we can decide that later."

"Or we can walk inside the box," Louie-Louie said. "We just use wheelchairs sometimes so we don't get too tired."

Mr. Kelly walked to the back of the store and came out carrying a big box. "How's this?"

"Too small," said Charlie, looking at Isabel.

"Yes, too small. Do you have another?"

Mr. Kelly smiled and took the box back. In a couple of minutes, he dragged a refrigerator box to the front of the store. "This OK?" He had a hopeful look on his face.

All the kids inspected it. The box might work, but it was fatter than it was tall. Isabel gave Mr. Kelly her most persuasive smile. "Could you look one more time? Something taller, or longer once we lay it down."

"I can help you look," offered Scott.

"Thanks, but I can't let customers in the back."

They watched Mr. Kelly drag the huge brown box back to the storeroom.

"I hope he's not losing patience with us," Avery said.

"No, he's awfully nice," Jadie said. "Maybe the next one will work."

"How about this really tall bookcase box? It's even taller than a refrigerator." Mr. Kelly tried to smile.

"Perfect." Isabel clapped her hands. "Thank you so much. Can we work in front of your store if we don't block the front door?"

"We might attract customers," Betsy pointed out. "They'd stop to see what we were doing, then come inside to see what you have."

"Sure. It probably won't take you long. Will it?"

"No, not long at all, since we're getting hungry." Chris laughed and slapped high fives, low fives, and some kind of secret handshake with Louie-Louie.

"Thanks a lot, Mr. Kelly," Isabel said. "You've been really nice to us. And we both know that you can't compromise when it comes to creativity."

Mr. Kelly melted again after Isabel smiled. "Here's a magic marker to get you started and an X-ACTO knife. You look like you can handle it, young man. It'll be easier to cut with a knife than scissors. Be careful, though." He passed the X-ACTO to Scott.

By the time Betsy got to the sidewalk in front of the store, they had opened up the box. Isabel had drawn a bus—wheels, windows, doors, the works. Scott was already slicing through the cardboard where Isabel indicated windows.

Charlie's mother and Jadie's mom had not helped with the project, but they'd watched proudly the whole time. It was clear that they wanted their children to have an adventure.

"Most parents and regular volunteers like me are trained to let the kids do as much as they can on their own," Betsy told Avery and Isabel softly. She smiled. "I like the way you just assumed the kids could do this, Isabel. You're a natural."

In a short time, watching Isabel draw and Scott cut, Chris announced. "It's a school bus! I used to hate riding the bus. Now I just wish I could go back to school."

Avery took going to school for granted. Maybe she wouldn't do that so much any more.

"The store had big bottles of tempura paint," Betsy said. "I'm going to take the scissors back and get two bottles of yellow paint and two brushes."

With everyone working, within a short time, they had a lovely car-bus-vehicle that met drive-thru standards. They had also drawn a crowd of onlookers. Most smiled and were patient with the sidewalk detour, and some even stopped to talk to the kids.

"What a fun project." "Why are you out here working on the sidewalk?" "Are you from the hospital?" Some made suggestions. Mr. Kelly eventually came out of the store to watch their progress and to offer a few pieces of advice.

The hospital kids were very friendly and vocal. They loved talking to people. Avery doubted all the cancer-ward kids had such ability to mix, but their foursome did. And she heard some of them tell the whole story, the why-they-had-to-make-a-car story.

From the corner of her eye, Avery saw a man with a camera taking photos and talking to the kids as well as the two mothers. She guessed that was all right. What they were doing certainly wasn't a secret.

"We could have made a yellow submarine," Louie-Louie said, grinning.

"No, this is a Hummer." Chris made motor noises. "Vroom, vroom."

"And it doesn't even use too much gas," Scott laughed.

"Don't you think we're being completely 'immature,' Avery?" Betsy said, reminding Avery of Anna's remark.

"Right on! Juvenile forever!" She and Isabel pumped their fists in the air, making up a new BSG motto.

Mr. Kelly applauded when he returned and saw the finished bus. "It's a Carrari," he said.

"No, it's a You-Can't-Stop-Us Mobile," Louie-Louie said, sticking his fist in the air.

Jadie wanted Scott to write that on the side of the car.

"Let's take a vote," he suggested. It was unanimous. The "You-Can't-Stop-Us Mobile" won hands down.

Betsy, who had even better handwriting than Isabel, lettered the slogan on the side of the car.

"It's a great vehicle. How are you going to get it back to

the drive-in?" Mr. Kelly asked.

"It'll be a little hard to carry, I guess," Scott said. "We'll have to wear it."

"It's my break time." Mr. Kelly looked at his watch. "I just might be in the mood for hamburgers and fries. And one of the delivery trucks is back. What if I sneaked it over to the restaurant and unloaded it where no one in the drive-thru could see it?"

"Thanks so much, Mr. Kelly!" Isabel enthused. Scott, Avery, Betsy, and all the kids echoed their thank yous.

By the time they walked back to Burger Stop, they were all starving. "I want a double cheeseburger with fries and a salad, with the yogurt fruit cup and some chocolate milk," Chris said, practically drooling as he spoke. As soon as Mr. Kelley pulled up, everybody became very efficient.

Louie-Louie was the strongest of the kids. He was going to walk. They lifted the box over the other three wheelchairs, resting the box sides just inside the wheels so it wouldn't drag.

"Ready?" Scott asked. He had tucked into the front, duck walking so he could see out the driver's side window, get the food, and hand over their money. They built the bus so that everyone had a window, but Avery, Isabel, and Betsy also had to duck walk. Louie-Louie only had to squash down a little.

They "drove" up to the very same girl as before.

"I'm so glad she wasn't on break," Avery whispered.

Giggles spread through the bus.

"That will be—hey!!" The girl in the window suddenly became speechless. Her face got red. "You can't ..."

Other employees ran to the window to look out. A man, the returned manager, the real boss, smiled. The You-Can't-Stop-Us-Mobile was in!

"Twenty-seven dollars and seventy-five cents." The girl

finished telling them how much they owed.

"Do we have enough?" Betsy asked. "I have the change from buying the paint." They all scrambled to count their crumpled dollar bills and change again.

The girl in the window took the money without saying another word.

They "drove" out of the pickup window, all the way in front and circled the restaurant to the picnic tables in the back. That was as far as they could walk with bent legs. Lifting the box, they realized that the man with the camera was still there.

"You're going to be on TV tonight, kids. Be sure to watch *All Around Boston* after the news." He shut down the camera, smiled and left.

"TV?" Avery looked at Isabel and Scott and Betsy.

"TV!" "Yeah!" "Right on." All the kids laughed while they dug into their sandwiches.

"I gave the reporter permission." Charlie's mother joined them. "I hope that's alright with everyone."

"Do we want to be on television turning a box into a car?" Avery whispered to Isabel.

Isabel grinned. "Definitely. I'm proud to be part of this very mature act." Both girls dissolved into laughter.

"Let's call the segment 'Mature Seventh Graders Help Out,'" said Betsy with a straight face.

They were all happily munching when Mr. Kelly offered a suggestion. "How about I deliver your Carrari up to the hospital? I'm sure it has some miles left in it."

"Yea," Charlie and the other kids clapped and cheered. "I want everyone to see it."

"Do you think they will be upset about the kids being on TV?" Avery said, a little worried that the hospital might not like all the publicity.

Avery was surprised to realize that she really did want to come back and work with the kids again. Maybe not build another car and get on television, but play games, talk to the kids. If Isabel came, she could give them some art lessons. Suddenly, the whole "party" thing seemed unimportant.

Marilyn was waiting for them at the entrance to the children's wing. "Do you think we're in serious trouble?" Avery whispered.

Marilyn stood there looking at them, hands on hips, painted clown smile frozen. "I think I see some very happy people here."

"I think they're going to be on television tonight," Charlie's mother told Marilyn. "I hope you don't mind."

"Sounds like good publicity. People need to see that kids are kids—no matter what. I hope you and Isabel come back again, Avery," Marilyn said.

"We will." Avery grinned at Isabel. "Most definitely."

"That *was* fun." Betsy's voice held a wistful tone.

"I have another good idea," Isabel said.

"Shoot." Avery dribbled her imaginary basketball and pushed in a rim shot.

"What if all the Beacon Street Girls came over to the hospital some Saturday and worked with the kids? We could dress like clowns," Isabel joked.

"I think clowns are creepy." Avery grimaced. "I have another idea. I saw a dog visiting some kids this morning. Let's teach Marty some more tricks and bring him to visit."

"Can I come too?" Betsy asked. "We can ask at the office, but I'm pretty sure that you have to get Marty specially trained."

"Sure," Avery and Isabel agreed together. Avery was starting to realize that even though Betsy's perfectionist tendencies were irritating, she was actually a really cool, smart person. And funny, too.

"They have a pet visiting program here. If you have a pet, especially a dog that is well behaved, he can visit the kids," Betsy continued.

"Hey, why can't we bring Marty when we're clowns? I could make him a little clown suit, and he could dance," Isabel suggested.

"Enough with the clowns." Avery laughed. "I'm going to teach Marty to do a hand ... no a *paw stand* on a basketball."

Chat Room: BSG

File Edit People View Help

4kicks: hey izzy, r u as tired as I am?

lafrida: yeah, kids are exhausting ... so fun 2 make those kids smile

4kicks: yup, can't wait 2 go back w/Marty. The kids would <3 him. Maybe we could bring everyone to the park & play fetch

lafrida: r u going back 2nite to help out?

4kicks: no ... mom said we all did enough volunteering 4 the day. she said to say thanks to u again

lafrida: de nada. So what r u gonna do 2nite?

4kicks: hang out and watch a movie with Scott. we're going 2 make popcorn and s'mores

lafrida: Elena let me off the hook, I owe her one. Mama's feeling good, so we r all going to that new Mexican restaurant

Chat Room: BSG

File Edit People View Help

4kicks: LOL ... How could I forget the baby-sitting fiasco?

lafrida: :-) But when she found out we were going out for dinner & she was gonna miss it, she pouted for almost an hour

4kicks: i believe it. truth time. do you wish you were going to the party instead?

lafrida: i guess it'd be fun, but I'm ok with not going. doesn't seem like such a big deal anymore

4kicks: yeah, i know whatcha mean. I think I'm over it ... and at least i don't have to get dressed up

lafrida: haha true. Well, have fun with scott+movies.

4kicks: thanx, hope the food's good ... TTYL

CHAPTER 14

DRESS REHEARSAL

MAEVE, Katani, and Charlotte had been on the phone or email all morning, so getting together at Charlotte's to talk and get dressed made sense. Maeve's mother had taken her on a fast shopping trip, so Maeve had a new top to wear.

After shopping, Maeve told her mom that she was going to run over to Irving's to pick up some Swedish Fish for the pre-party at Charlotte's. Mrs. Weiss and Swedish Fish were two of Maeve's favorites. When she got there, Mrs. Weiss looked up from her seat next to the candy display and smiled. Maeve was blowing on her still wet nails that she had manicured in the car.

"Going somewhere special?" Mrs. Weiss asked.

"Big party tonight, Mrs. Weiss," Maeve said , waving her fingers back and forth a few times before picking up the Swedish Fish.

"Well, have a wonderful time, and be careful," Mrs. Weiss said, handing Maeve change for a five dollar bill. "You never know ..."

"I will see you soon, Mrs. Weiss, thanks for the Fish!"

✿

Maeve opened the door and speed-walked home, thoughts of the party racing through her head. She ran up the apartment stairs and pulled out her Think Pink bag to organize her stuff for the evening.

"Do you have everything, sweetie?" Maeve's mother said as she put her things in the car. "Sam and I are going to get something to eat and then go to a movie. I won't be home until closer to the time the party should be over."

"We're seeing *Young Frankenstein* at the horror flick festival," Sam said. "Remember, it's really funny."

"Yes, Sam, I remember. And I'm ready, Mom. I could probably borrow from Katani or Charlotte if I put my outfit on and it's all wrong."

"Have a good time tonight, Maeve. No worrying about school, math, or anything else. OK? Promise?" Her mother smiled at her and waved. "Then, Monday you start on your new schedule."

Maeve sighed. She wondered how long it was going to be before her mother remembered schedules. Her mother loved schedules. Maeve figured she was born that way. Maeve, on the other hand, found schedules to be a burden. They always had you paying attention to something that interfered with the excitement of the moment.

"I'm totally thrilled about the party, aren't you, Charlotte?" Maeve said when Charlotte answered the door.

Maeve would have knocked and gone on in, but her arms were loaded. She had brought a suitcase of emergency stuff.

"Are you moving in, Maeve?" Charlotte laughed.

"I had to have choices." Maeve dumped her things in Charlotte's bedroom and danced around the room with Marty.

Katani hurried into Charlotte's room five minutes after Maeve. "Wait 'til you see what I did to my shoes. You're going to want me to make some for both of you."

"Let's see." Maeve hurried to help Katani. "Did you paint them?"

Katani pulled out a pair of stone-pink, suede flats. "I found these shoes at Filene's bargain basement. They were cheap but pretty plain. Then when I was upstairs I saw a pair the exact same color, except the expensive pair was decorated. I mean, the upstairs pair cost $350 dollars."

"You paid $350 dollars for a pair of flats for the party," Charlotte gasped.

"No way, Charlotte. I just saw them upstairs and made the basement shoes to look like upstairs shoes. I realized I could decorate my own, so I raced back downstairs before someone grabbed up the bargain pair," Katani explained.

"Wow, Katani, you are so creative." Charlotte took the *Kgirl* pair and looked them over.

"And a really smart shopper," piped in Maeve.

Across the toes, with wine-colored paint and sequins, Katani had fashioned flowers, dotted them with sequins, and then painted dark green vines around them. For accent, she had outlined everything, including the flower petals, with a thin line of gold paint.

"These are like totally vogue," Maeve said. "You're right, I have to have a pair. What are you wearing, Charlotte? Are they heels?"

Charlotte shook her head. "No way."

Katani walked over to where Charlotte had her new top, her shoes, and her bracelets laid out. "I guessed right, Char.

You're wearing plain black flats."

Maeve laughed. "Those are so in right now. Very Audrey Hepburnish ... You know," she added when she saw Charlotte's quizzical look "... *Breakfast at Tiffany's*."

"Wow, I'm a fashion winner." Charlotte laughed at Maeve's theatrics. "But don't you think they're a little bit boring for a hula party?"

"Not totally, but in case you want to jazz it up, I brought a miracle cure for plain shoes." Katani pulled a pair of butterflies from her overnight case. "I made these. You'll wear them, and it'll be like free advertising. Everyone will want some."

"Shoe clips. How clever." Charlotte took the clips from Katani, and sure enough, they fit right on the flats. "My shoes have been transformed! How'd you make these?"

"I used a scrap of crinoline. I had gotten a piece to make a petticoat so I'd have one of those new bell skirts. I just cut it into the shape of a butterfly, sprayed it with some gold paint, and added gold sequins."

"I love these, Katani. They're magical. And they look great with my top." Charlotte put on her shoes and felt as if her feet would float like a butterfly. "I can dance without worrying about stepping on anyone's toes. I'll be really careful and give them back after the party."

"No, they're yours. They cost me almost nothing to make. But if anyone asks where you got them, say she can order a pair from me. I'm going to make butterflies, lady bugs, and maybe some flowers."

"I think you should do fruit, too. Everyone loves cherries and strawberries," Maeve added.

"Great idea. I'll offer those too."

"Clip them on a card, Katani, and stamp the card with your logos. Put each pair in a Ziplock bag, and charge at least five dollars." Charlotte spun around the room, bumped into a chair, and had to catch herself to keep from falling.

Marty barked and jumped and danced on his hind legs. He was so happy to have the girls together, not knowing they were going to leave as soon as they got dressed.

"Marty loves butterflies," Maeve laughed. "Guys, don't you feel just a little bit guilty that there aren't five of us here getting dressed?"

"Yeah, but I got an IM from Avery earlier that said she was helping her mother at the hospital. So she found something to do. I'd feel horrible if I knew she was sitting home." Katani laid out her makeup.

"Charlotte," Mr. Ramsey called out. "Come here. Hurry. There's going to be a story on the evening news you girls might want to see."

"TV? We don't have time to watch TV. Char ..."

"Dad wouldn't have called us if it wasn't important." Charlotte headed out of her room toward the living area and the television set.

"Hurry, they just showed a preview clip." Mr. Ramsey moved so all three girls could sit on the couch.

Suddenly a familiar face appeared on the screen.

"Avery, that's Avery!" Maeve squealed.

"And Isabel," Charlotte added.

"And—and Betsy. What are they doing?" Katani's eyes got wide as she watched and listened. Then she started to laugh.

The clip was long enough to tell the whole story of the kids from the hospital making a car so they could go through the drive-thru window at the fast food restaurant.

"I love it! They're famous. Not only did they find something to do today, they got the story on the news. I can hardly wait to hear every word of what happened from

✿

Isabel and Avery." Charlotte grinned. "Thanks, Dad. We would have missed it if you hadn't called us in."

"So much for worrying that they were sitting home bummed out," Katani said, leading the way back to Charlotte's room.

"Wait until we tell all the kids tonight. The Queens of Mean are going to be so jealous," Maeve said, pleased that her excluded friend would not be considered a loser. "But what about our TV star friends? We have to let them know we're their biggest fans. Let's send them an email."

> You two are famous and the best. We love the car and you both look like TV stars. Katani, Charlotte and Maeve.

"OK, let's get glamorous." Katani stepped away from the computer and pulled out her makeup kit. Katani loved putting makeup on her friends. It was so rewarding to enhance their best features. It was almost like being a painter.

Katani decided that Maeve's makeup should be done in peach tones, which would play up her natural redhead skin tone. Just for a special effect, she painted a little peach on Maeve's cheekbone.

"Katani, I look completely fabulous!" Maeve's grin was a mile wide as she looked in the mirror.

When it was Charlotte's turn, she whispered to Katani, "No peach for me."

Katani was insulted. "Charlotte, I never make two faces up the same way. I'll just do a little dab of rose colored blush and soft lip gloss." Charlotte felt bad that she had ruffled Katani's feathers, but she was a low-maintenance kind of girl. She wanted to look special for the party, but she would feel foolish if she was flashy. Maeve could be flashy. That was her style. Not Charlotte's.

"Do you think we'll get to dance?" Katani asked.

"Absolutely. What's a party without dancing?" Maeve practiced a few steps.

"You look like America's Next Top Model," Charlotte added. "Alongside you, I feel as if I'm about 8 years old."

"You are losing the pigtails." Quickly, Katani pulled out her friend's pigtails, and with a gleeful smile, turned her curling iron to Charlotte's hair. Like magic, Charlotte's hair fell in soft waves around her face. "Voilà!" Katani smiled.

"Charlotte, you look amazing!" exclaimed Maeve. Charlotte had to admit Katani had done everything just right. Not over the top glam, but enough to transform Charlotte from frazzled Abigail Adams student newspaper feature writer to oh-so-cool party goer. Charlotte was pleased. She blushed when she realized she was wondering what Nick Montoya would think.

All three of the girls were wearing jeans, but Katani was wearing a gold satin top with spaghetti straps. She made a little cropped gold brocade jacket to wear as well. Along with her big hoop earrings, she looked very exotic.

"How much longer?" Mr. Ramsey called through the door. "The party will be over before you girls even get there."

Laughing, they tumbled out of Charlotte's room. They each strutted down a pretend model runway for Charlotte's dad. He clapped his hands and in a perfect imitation of a British accent pronounced: "Absolutely smashing."

Maeve giggled and decided that she was going to use the word "smashing" more often.

CHAPTER 15

PARTY TIME

THE FABERS' HOUSE was lit up like a Hawaiian Disneyland. There were a million white lights on the picket fences that surrounded the house. Palm trees lined the front walk, strung with pink and lime green lights. Hula music floated from a CD player set on the porch. A young woman dressed in a grass skirt waited to toss a lei of fresh flowers over each girl's head. The most popular kids in the seventh grade were there, and Katani had to admit that their presence gave the party that "special star quality." She felt a little special herself, and then felt a twinge of guilt because Avery had been excluded. Life was so complicated sometimes, Katani sighed. But the surrounding sparkle quickly drew her attention back into party mode.

"Look at the palm trees!" Charlotte said. "They're real."

"They're in pots. You can probably rent them from some nursery in town," Katani stated.

Maeve was completely transfixed by the effect. This was going to be a fabulous party. She could just feel it in her bones.

"You can rent palm trees?" Charlotte stored up that

information for future reference. Oh yes, I'd like to rent five palm trees, please. They're for a Tower room. How soon can you have them here? She giggled at the idea.

Pink flamingos covered in lights lined the walk, as well.

"Are there flamingos in Hawaii?" Katani asked.

"I know they have them in Africa, and I think, Florida," Charlotte replied. "I don't know about Hawaii."

"Are you going to sit in the car all night, or go see what's going on inside?" Mr. Ramsey joked. "Maybe I could sneak in, just to see for myself?"

"Please, Dad, no." Charlotte leaned over and hugged him. "I'll tell you all about it on the way home tonight."

Maeve got out of the car and started moving right away. She did a hula dance right to the door.

"Call when you want to come home, Charlotte. The party is over at 11:00, right? I'll read or grade papers until then."

Charlotte nodded and waved, then walked to the door with Katani. She could feel her party butterflies beginning.

"Do you think Nick and the other guys are here yet?" asked Katani.

"He said he'd be here right when it started." Charlotte inhaled the perfume of the flowered necklace she'd been given. Suddenly, she was transported to a beautiful Hawaiian beach, surfers riding the big wave and beautiful Hawaiian women handing out beautiful flowers. The Fabers put up a big screen with projected images of Hawaii, which you could see through the big picture window. It looked so dreamy. Maybe she and her father would have to travel there soon.

They didn't bother ringing the bell, since the woman at the door said to go on in. The music from downstairs was too loud anyway.

But when they walked inside and down to the huge family

✿

room in the basement, almost cleared of furniture, the party wasn't exactly raving. No one was dancing. In fact, it was vaguely similar to the first party of the year at Abigail Adams Junior High. Girls were standing on one side of the room. Boys hung out on the other side, looking at the refreshment table. Some had grabbed a soda before they froze into zombies. Others stood, hands hanging at their sides like dead fish.

"Hey, they need us to liven things up," Maeve whispered.

"I bet Julie wishes you-know-who was here right now," asserted Katani. Avery would have everybody going in a second.

Julie Faber's face was set in an icy pout. Girls hovered around her, but she acted as if she had no idea what to do.

Chelsea Briggs stood near the refreshment table, ready to take photos. She wasn't dressed in party clothes, just black pants and a wine-colored T-shirt.

"Get any photos yet?" Charlotte asked. "Be sure to get pictures of the entrance with all those palm trees and pink flamingos. It's really amazing!"

Chelsea grinned. "Yeah, I got a couple of good shots of the entrance. Now I'm waiting for something to happen that's worth a photo here. Slow start, I'd say."

Maeve, Katani, and Charlotte moved closer to Julie's circle. Charlotte looked at Katani, who shrugged. Maeve's eyes searched the room, looking for Dillon. "Do you see Nick and Dillon?" she whispered.

"Nope, only Henry Yurt, our famous class president, and Pete Wexler, super JV football star," Katani said. "They're just standing around, too."

Julie whispered, but loud enough for the BSG minus two to hear. "Why isn't this working? I invited all the popular kids. Kids who know how to have fun. What can I do?"

None of Julie's friends had any answer to her dilemma.

"There!" Maeve pointed. "Dillon and Nick are here. Finally. Let's take them a can of soda before they get trapped on the boys' side."

All three girls grabbed an extra soda and headed for Nick and Dillon.

As soon as Nick spotted Charlotte his face lit up.

"Hey," he said, but didn't get to finish the sentence.

Despite Charlotte's wearing flats and there not being even one rug on the floor, she managed to trip over a speck of dust, a missed dust bunny, or maybe her own foot, which was supposed to be light as a butterfly. "Oh!" she squealed. "Oh, no!" Half the open soda she carried jetted into the air and came straight down onto the front of Nick's sweater.

Being the gentleman that he was, Nick caught Charlotte before she sprawled onto the floor.

"Hi, Charlotte," he said. "Trying to liven up the party?"

"Oh, Nick, I ... I'm so sorry. I'm—"

"Going to get a bunch of napkins before the dance floor gets sticky?"

"Yes, yes, right. I'll get several." Charlotte spun around and hurried back to the big table which was laden with sliced pineapple, chunks of fresh coconut, and little cups of fruit salad. She grabbed a handful of the palm-tree covered paper napkins and hurried back to Nick.

By that time, his sweater had absorbed all the soda. All she could do was dab at the damp wool.

"I told Mom I didn't need a sweater tonight." Nick whipped off the sweater. "I'll just take it off. It's hot in here anyway. Is it supposed to *feel* like a tropical island?"

It *was* hot in the basement. Part of the heat was in Charlotte's cheeks and lungs as she tried to breathe normally.

✿

"I'll be right back." She ran in the direction of a hall that might have a bathroom. Maeve and Katani hurried right behind her.

"So embarrassing. Right at the beginning of the party. Why do I do things like that?"

"You wanted to fall into Nick's arms?" Katani looked at the mirror to make sure her own makeup wasn't smeared.

Now Charlotte giggled. "I didn't even get to stay in his arms that long."

"You can't blame it on high heels," Katani laughed. "Look at it this way. Maybe you got the party to loosen up a little. I did hear a lot of people laughing."

"Yeah, right." Charlotte would have hidden in the bathroom the rest of the night, but Katani and Maeve pushed her back out into the hall and then into the party room.

Someone had put on a CD of some slower Hawaiian music, and Yurt and Anna were dancing. Had Yurt grown a couple of inches overnight? He was almost as tall as Anna. Little by little, other couples joined them.

A voice behind Charlotte asked, "Want to dance?"

"That's risky." Charlotte turned around without looking at Nick.

"I'll take the chance." He held her at enough distance that she could look at his feet and breathe. Charlotte was about to risk looking into his eyes, when Mrs. Faber stopped the music and spoke in a loud voice.

"Welcome, everyone, to Julie's thirteenth birthday party. Thank you all for coming. And now, Mr. Faber and I have a big surprise. Julie didn't even know we were doing this. We have invited a live band as part of the entertainment. Please give Mustard Monkey a big welcome."

Mrs. Faber stepped aside as Riley Lee and the Mustard

Monkeys came into the room carrying guitars, drums, loud speakers, and a microphone.

"Riley Lee?" Julie said, right behind Nick and Charlotte. "I didn't invite Riley. It's my party. I didn't know I could have a live band. I can't believe my mother did this."

A live band was really special. Charlotte thought Julie sounded awfully spoiled. As soon as Riley got set up and started to play, the party began to loosen up. Riley knew what he was doing. He played some old-time rock 'n' roll that got everyone up and going. Peter Wexler and Dillon, who were really fabulous dancers, started parading across the floor like rock stars. They pretended they had guitars and were performing for the crowd. Their antics succeeded in getting the party really hopping. The boys clapped and acted goofy and enticed the girls to dance. Julie's icy pout had turned into a beaming smile. Charlotte guessed it would be really difficult to throw a party and have everybody act like it was boring.

"Did you know Riley was coming, Maeve?" Charlotte whispered as she, Katani, and Maeve danced in a big group.

"Are you singing?" Katani asked. "And you didn't even tell us. No wonder it was so important to have a new outfit."

"I had no idea," Maeve shook her head, denying keeping a secret from Charlotte and Katani. "And, no, I'm not singing."

"Mustard Monkey may be just what the party needs," Katani smiled.

"Go, Riley," Maeve said, as she and Charlotte stepped close to Nick and Dillon. "How about some hula music with a rapper beat?"

Charlotte enjoyed Maeve's enthusiasm, but when she looked at Dillon, she could see that not everyone at the party was so glad to see Riley Lee. Dillon was definitely jealous of Riley. Riley was talented and had a big crush on Maeve. Her sparkly, friendly personality made it so fun to be around her. And the red hair ... even the boys knew that there was something special about red hair. Now Dillon and Riley stared at each other, each wishing the other were somewhere else.

CHAPTER 16

CRASH

"JUST THINK," Charlotte whispered, "Riley Lee got his start writing a music column for the newspaper. Look at him now."

"Yeah, he's gotten really awesome," Maeve said. "But he's been taking music lessons for years, and he practices all the time. He's a really dedicated musician." Charlotte could tell that Maeve really admired Riley.

"This is still a secret, but Riley suggested I help him write lyrics to some of his original music." Charlotte thought it would be fun to hear some of her poetry set to music.

"You're kidding." Katani looked at Charlotte. "You gave him some stuff, didn't you?"

"A few things. He told me they were getting more gigs than they can handle, and he doesn't have time to write lyrics. But, he likes to do original music to stand out."

Riley hadn't said anything more about using Charlotte's poems, though, even the last one she'd given him. She assumed he didn't like it, or it didn't qualify for music lyrics. In fact, she'd gotten so busy, she had forgotten about what he was doing until he performed at the election dance. And, lo and behold, Maeve had shown up, singing one of Riley's songs with the band.

The band had graduated from jeans to hip hop baggy pants and mustard-colored T-shirts with monkeys printed on the back. Riley cut his long hair and now had it styled so it stuck up all over his head. Charlotte was impressed with Riley for taking the chance to do something he believed in. And for not letting anyone tell him he couldn't start a band.

Chelsea Briggs snapped some photos as soon as the band got going.

Riley didn't play much rap music. Charlotte happened to know that Riley was a hard-core rock fan. A song that Riley had written called *Baby Blue Eyes* had an awesome beat—enough to really get the party loosened up.

Dillon grabbed Maeve and pulled her onto the dance floor. Nick danced with Charlotte. Henry Yurt pulled Anna out to try to keep up with him. Some people were still content to watch, but Charlotte smiled to see Pete Wexler invite Katani out onto the floor. Charlotte knew Katani, as popular as she was, could also be shy, especially around boys. But Pete was so outgoing, he'd get her talking to him.

Riley played two other numbers that had everyone sweating. A master of timing, Riley slowed the pace down and took the mike. "Since this is Julie's birthday, we have to have a birthday song. But since Julie's theme is Hawaiian, I've chosen tonight to introduce a new ballad, the words written by someone who is here tonight. She calls the piece 'Lonely Nights are the Same All over the World.'"

Charlotte caught her breath and held it until she felt light-headed. This was her poem! The one she thought Riley had forgotten about or maybe even thrown out. Hardly aware, she gripped Nick's hand tightly.

Full moon shines in the Outback,
You wake in your tent alone.
A kookaburra laughs at empty dreams,
His voice leaves a haunting tone.

The orange cat strays at midnight,
Rain mist hides her escape.
You search alone, clothed in fog,
Wonder what path to take.

Beach waves pull me to you,
Safe shadows whisper, "Hide."
Friends are pulled from beneath your feet
And wash out on the tide.

The world thinks you are sleeping.
You cannot close your eyes.
For you the day is safer.
You need blue sunshine skies,
You need blue sunshine skies.

Riley nodded to Charlotte, without saying her name or introducing her, thank goodness. Nick put an arm around her shoulders.

"Charlotte ... your song ..." Katani said. "It's wonderful."

"Are you crying, Char?" Maeve hugged Charlotte. "That was beautiful. I wish he could sing it again."

The rest of the room was silent, and obviously Riley had chosen to end his set with that piece.

Julie exploded. "Oh! Riley played someone else's song at my party? Why didn't he play a song for me at my own party?" Julie had forgotten he'd dedicated a song to her. Riley probably hadn't realized that singing Charlotte's ballad at the party would upset Julie.

"How rude! Riley does something nice for her and Julie totally ranks him out. I can't believe it!" Katani exclaimed.

"What should I do?" Charlotte turned to her friends. "Riley probably didn't realize he was going to upset her."

"There's nothing you can do, Charlotte," Nick said. "Just enjoy that your words were set to music. Julie will be OK in a minute. She's a drama queen. You know, she loves all the attention!"

Charlotte was surprised at how insightful Nick was. Julie did like drama. It was probably why she didn't invite Avery—because she knew everyone would be talking about Julie, the party, and who was coming and who wasn't for weeks.

It was comforting for Charlotte to be friends with a boy who seemed so aware of how other people really were. She could have danced with Nick Montoya forever. And maybe Riley should have played one more slow number, or any kind of song to finish. Instead, the band looked as if they were leaving.

"Stay for the party, of course, Riley," Julie said, recovering from her anger. She ran over to Riley. Maybe she realized that Riley and his band had saved a sinking ship. "And plan to play some more. I'm so glad my parents invited you." Julie probably hoped her fake enthusiasm made up for her earlier rudeness. Riley looked confused. He didn't understand girls like Julie. One minute, they acted one way, the next minute, another. Riley shook his head.

"But Riley," squealed Julie, "you can't leave before cake."

But Mrs. Faber was coming down the stairs carrying a huge birthday cake with pink coconut frosting, Hawaiian figures on the top, and HAPPY BIRTHDAY spelled out with pink icing. Mr. Faber followed with several buckets of ice cream. Choices of flavor were coconut, mango, pineapple, and strawberry. Riley and the band decided to stay. After all, cake was cake!

Julie looked half embarrassed, half pleased when everyone gathered around, sang, and watched her blow out fourteen candles—one to grow on—which took her two tries, and a half dozen photo opportunities.

"You left two candles. You won't get your wish for two years!" Anna McMasters teased.

After Mrs. Faber cut the cake, served the ice cream, and made sure everyone had plenty to eat, she and Mr. Faber went back upstairs to their own party.

"Where's Maeve?" Charlotte asked Katani.

Katani nodded her head toward where the band had performed. Maeve had left Dillon with them and was laughing and talking with Riley Lee and two more Mustard Monkeys. Dillon was watching Maeve, and it didn't take a mind reader to tell that he was jealous.

"Hey, Dillon," Henry Yurt said, not even trying to keep his voice low. "Maybe you need to start a band."

"Chill out," Katani said to the boys. "Maeve can talk to anyone she wants." Katani grabbed Charlotte's hand. "It's time for a break."

Katani and Charlotte scooped up Maeve by each arm and headed up the stairs, looking for another bathroom. The house was big enough to have several.

"Hey, what are you doing?" Maeve asked, trying to shake off her captors.

"Riley needed to play another set. And we need to talk."

As soon as they found another bathroom, this one twice as big as the one downstairs, Katani said, "Dillon is jealous."

✿

"Well, I'm sorry." Maeve put her hands on her hips. "Has he invited me to a movie or anything since we went to the basketball game? No. And what kind of date is one where his father and his big brother go along and all of them totally ignore me?"

"Wow," Charlotte said, putting up both hands. "Calm down, Maeve."

"I'm calm!" Maeve let herself out of the bathroom, slamming the door behind her.

"She's right," Katani said. "She and Dillon aren't together. And even if they were, she could talk to other people."

By the time Charlotte and Katani got back to the basement rec room, Riley and the band were playing again. Someone had started the Hershey Mitten Game. A hold-over from sixth grade, the Hershey Mitten Game continued to be a huge fave with Abigail Adams chocolate fanatics, which was just about everyone.

"How do you play?" Charlotte asked Katani as they watched. She had never heard of the game.

In the center of a table sat a huge Hershey's chocolate bar.

Katani explained. "It's cool. People take turns rolling dice until someone rolls a double. Whoever rolls a double puts on a knit hat, a scarf, and a pair of mittens."

About that time, Pete rolled a double. As soon as he had on the hat and scarf and mittens, he cut a piece of chocolate off the big bar with a knife and fork and started eating. Soon a big chocolate smile spread across his face. Chelsea snapped a photo, either for Julie's photo album or for blackmail, or maybe both. Although the way Pete was laughing, he probably didn't care who saw the picture.

"My turn." When Maeve rolled a double, she took the hat, scarf, and mittens from Pete and put them on. She cut off another piece of chocolate and chewed fast.

"Whoever eats the last piece of chocolate wins." Katani laughed. "And is sick. Want to play, Char?"

"I think I'd rather dance." Charlotte waved at Riley, who nodded to her and smiled. Then she looked around for Nick, but he seemed to have disappeared. A boy named Andy, who she didn't know well, asked her to dance. Her father told her once that it was sometimes really hard for a boy to get up the courage to ask a girl to dance. So, if she felt comfortable, she should try to honor the request. Right then it was OK with her. She really liked the song and wanted to dance some more.

While they spun around the room, Charlotte heard the crowd cheering Maeve on. "Go Maeve go! Go Maeve go!"

Charlotte stumbled over the boy's foot and was about to apologize when Nick cut in. "I agree with you, Char. I think I'd rather dance." He grinned as the music got faster and they bounced to keep up.

Riley and his band paused between numbers just as Charlotte and Nick, and Katani and Pete reached the far end of the room. A door opened right beside them. Cool air suggested it led to a garage and then outside.

Five boys busted into the room, laughing, talking, and pushing each other. Charlotte smelled something funny as they walked past.

"Is that beer I smell?" she asked Nick.

"I think so." Nick looked worried.

One of the boys was swigging from a Coke can. Charlotte's dad had warned her that some kids put liquor in soda cans to hide it from grown-ups. "Uh-oh," Pete said, putting his arm around Katani and pulling her farther into the corner. "This could be trouble."

Nick and Charlotte moved back against the wall. "Who

is that?" Charlotte asked.

"Julie's brother Bobby and Tim Cole, and some other boys I don't know," Katani said.

"They're eighth graders, right? They look like trouble."

"Yeah. They're acting really stupid. Julie looks like she's going to explode," Katani said. "Remember what Elena said about them?"

Charlotte's eyes met Katani's, and then both of them turned to watch what was going on.

The boys were fake wrestling with each other and knocking things over. Tim drop-kicked his empty Coke can, which smashed into the wall.

"What do you think we should do?" Charlotte asked.

"Nothing ... for now," Nick advised. "Julie must know how to handle her own brother. Or maybe they won't want to stay at a seventh-grade party."

Not so.

"Look, I told you guys this would be a blast. Look at the babies eating chocolate with mittens on. And look who thinks he can have a band. It's Riley and the mustard boys."

Bobby, who was a big kid, grabbed Riley around the head and gave him a noogie. Riley wrestled to get away. "Hey, let go."

Bobby laughed and headed across the room, walking with a swagger. His buddies followed, calling out insults to anyone who'd listen.

And the party had stopped. Everyone had frozen like statues, listening and watching to see what would happen next.

CHAPTER 17

ơ

CAKE, ICE CREAM, AND A LITTLE SOMETHING EXTRA

"BOBBY," JULIE SAID, her voice wavering. "I'm going to tell Mom. You're not supposed to be here. This is my party." She stamped her foot at her brother for emphasis.

"But, Jules," he goofed on his sister, "I missed the hula cake and ice cream and the really mature mitten game. Besides," he looked around at the rather subdued atmosphere, "it looks to me like this party needs some attitude … you know, a little action." Bobby looked for and got the backup comments he wanted from his too-cool-for-words eighth-grade buddies. To Maeve's surprise, one of the gang included Tim Cole, her favorite hip hop partner. Tim was an eighth grader, but she hadn't known that he was a friend of Bobby Faber's. Things were looking up, thought Maeve. This party had been a little boring.

"Yeah, so how's it going, Jules? Let's dance!" Larry Parker took Julie's arm and pulled her out in a clear space to dance. "Why has the band stopped playing? Play, Mustard Boys." He waved his arm like a band director.

Riley glared at him, and then turned to look at his band.

He gave the signal to start another number. He didn't much care about Julie's party, but these guys looked like they were just looking for trouble. Riley scanned the room, and he noticed that Dillon, Pete Wexler, and Billy Trentini were looking a little weirded out as well. "Geesh," Riley whispered to his band. He felt a little hot all of a sudden.

"Julie has a serious crush on Larry," one of Julie's friends whispered to Charlotte. "I'm sure I don't know why. He's such a loser. So is Bobby. They think they're so cool 'cause their soccer team has the best record in the city. But they're so not. They're totally annoying," the girl added.

Katani asked, "Should we go get Julie's parents?"

"I think that's up to Julie," Charlotte said. "It's her party. But maybe we should leave. Shall I call my dad?"

"Let's see what Maeve thinks. I'll go get her." Katani made her way through the crowd, her parents' warning running through her head, "Any sign of trouble, you come home immediately." Katani found Maeve hanging around the refreshment table, chatting with several girls from their class.

"Charlotte and I think we should go, Maeve. These eighth-grade boys aren't supposed to be here, and they're acting kind of funny. Let's get going, OK?"

"Leave? Now? It's just getting fun. Tim Cole just asked me to dance."

"Tim Cole?" Katani stayed right beside Maeve.

"Tim's in my hip hop dance class. He's not only the cutest guy in the class, he's the best dancer. Besides me, of course." Maeve smiled at Tim, who was walking toward them.

"But Maeve—" Charlotte, who had walked over to join them, watched Tim smile at Maeve. He was cute, Charlotte had to admit. But something just didn't feel right. Tim smelled like beer when he walked past Charlotte.

"It's OK. Chill, you guys. I'll be fine, just go back to Nick and Pete."

"What about Dillon?" Katani said.

Maeve walked away so fast she didn't hear Katani.

She joined Tim, who was already showing off some of the latest moves. She tapped him on the arm, flashed a smile, and began dancing … following Tim's lead some of the time, but challenging him with her own style, too. The music got faster. Maeve and Tim matched their steps to the bouncing beat. Soon a small group surrounded them to watch their moves. Maeve was in her element. But Tim … Maeve could see that his dancing was a little sloppy. What was the matter with him?

The next minute, Tim stumbled and almost fell. He laughed to cover his clumsiness and took Maeve's arm, pulling her off the dance floor.

"I need to rest, Maeve. That's hard work." Tim laughed and leaned on the refreshment table, almost losing his balance in the process.

Maeve caught her breath, but was sorry to stop dancing. She felt as if she could dance all night. Especially with Tim. It seemed weird to stop all of a sudden. She'd seen Tim Cole dance for an entire hour at class before.

"Could you get me a glass of water?" Tim wiped his brow and then the rest of his face with a palm-tree napkin. "I don't feel so well."

Maeve poured punch into a cup, since she didn't see any water. The punch was very sweet, but it was wet. She hurried back to Tim.

"Here, I didn't see any water, but have some punch. Are you OK?"

"Sure, Maeve. Why wouldn't I be OK? You're OK, too, you know. You look really great tonight." He reached over and grabbed one of her curls. "Pretty hair, I'll be ready to dance again in a minute."

Tim took the cup of punch with one hand and Maeve's arm with the other. He held onto her arm while he tossed back the sweet liquid, then he burped. "Whoa, that's better."

Now closer to Tim, Maeve wrinkled her nose. "Ugh, what's that smell? Have you been drinking? That is so gross." Maeve started to walk away.

"Wait, Maeve. Want to go to a movie with me tomorrow night?" Tim grabbed Maeve's arm and pulled her to a corner, away from the other kids.

How funny for Tim to invite her to a movie, since she lived over the movie theater and could see any show any time she liked. But even if that wasn't the case, she didn't think she wanted to go any place with Tim. He wasn't who she thought he was.

"I don't go out with boys who drink. It's dumb. We are only 12, for goodness sakes. It's not one bit cool or legal. And it kills brain cells. Don't you know that?" Maeve was starting to feel really mad. She had thought Tim was something special. Now she just wanted to get away from him. She should have listened to Katani and Charlotte and left the party.

"Well, Miss Goody-Goody. You think you're too good to go out with me, don't you? Miss Popular. I take it back. You're not half as cute as you think you are." A shocked Maeve turned to give him a piece of her mind when his face suddenly turned ashen. Gripping the side of the table, he began to raise his hand to his mouth. What happened next Billy Trentini described later as "truly gruesome—like something out of a horror movie. I mean, Cole spewed everywhere. It was like a geyser."

Chunks of pepperoni pizza and red punch flew out of

"Let's bolt … now." A shaken Katani grabbed Charlotte's hand and headed toward the stairs.

Maeve couldn't wait to leave the party now. She ran to follow Katani and Charlotte. "Charlotte, call your dad to come and get us. Someone should have a cell phone," she said in a panicked voice.

Chelsea, who had raced across the room to join them, handed Charlotte her cell phone. "Use mine. I'm getting out of here, too."

Charlotte grabbed the phone and flicked it open. "Thanks, Chels."

When her dad answered the phone, Charlotte said, "Did you walk Marty tonight? … OK, thanks, bye Dad," and then hung up.

"What was that all about?" Nick asked. "You didn't tell him to come pick you up."

"My dad and I made up a code phrase to use. He heard from some other parent that it's a good idea … so kids can feel OK about calling their parents for help and not worry about what other people think," Charlotte explained.

"That's a good idea. I should tell my mom about that … maybe ours could be 'Don't forget to bake the muffins for tomorrow morning,'" Nick joked. "I'm leaving too. "Can I catch a ride?"

"Sure." Charlotte didn't want any of her friends to stay. Who knows what could happen next? She didn't even want to think about it.

A line of fellow party deserters followed, a conga line oozing its way up the stairs—Charlotte, followed by Nick, Maeve and a wounded Dillon, then Katani, who was surprised when Pete took her hand and came along behind her.

✿

They hurried up the stairs to the second floor.

"Mrs. Faber!" Charlotte shouted over the TV volume, which seemed to be at full volume.

"Why girls, and boys," Mrs. Faber acknowledged the male members of the huddle of BSG and friends. "Are you leaving already? Aren't you having fun?"

"Thank you for the great party, Mrs. Faber," Charlotte said. "I told my father we wouldn't stay out late."

Quickly, the group went outside on the Fabers' lawn to wait for him. The palm trees swayed in a slight wind, the lights twinkled, and the pink flamingos looked out of place in Brookline, far from their habitat. The Hawaiian music was quiet, and the girl handing out leis had long gone home or inside someplace. Nobody said a word.

"Wait a minute. Where is Katani?"

Nick pointed to Katani racing across the lawn. "Here she comes; she must have stopped to get her jacket."

"Julie was really upset," said Charlotte in a subdued tone.

"Do you blame her? You only get to turn thirteen once." Maeve raked her hand through a palm tree frond.

"The Fabers should have made sure Bobby had something to do tonight," Nick said. "They have to know that their own kid is major trouble."

"Yeah, I heard Julie tell Kiki that she had asked him to stay away, so she knew he could cause problems. Oh, there's my brother. I'll see you Monday." Chelsea turned and grinned at the group. "I don't think Tim Cole will be in school on Monday." She sprinted off with a backward wave.

"You know," commented Pete to Katani, "Chelsea looks kinda different."

"Yeah, she really does," a breathy Katani answered.

Charlotte hoped her father got there fast. She felt funny

huddled in front of the house, randomly chatting about Chelsea, while Dillon's eye turned a disgusting green color, Katani's normally take-charge personality shrunk away, and Maeve, the "Chatty Kathy" of the group, had stopped talking altogether. The party lights all looked rather lonely now, twinkling in the cold air.

Maeve glanced at Dillon's eye. She hoped he would forgive her. But, really, it wasn't her fault. She wasn't the one who had started anything. *I just wanted to dance,* she thought to herself.

Kids were beginning to pour out of Julie's house. Some were running across the lawn.

Luckily, Charlotte's father pulled up in front and got out of his car. "I didn't expect you to call for another hour or more."

"Dad, do you think we can fit all of us in the car?" Charlotte said. "I'll tell you what happened later."

Mr. Ramsey hesitated as he noticed Dillon's eye. "Well, we'll be breaking the seat belt law, but all right. Pile in. You kids OK? You want to stop at J.P. Licks ... get some ice cream?"

The ice cream shop was packed. It seemed that everyone who was not at Julie's was slurping down on ice cream tonight. Mr. Ramsey suggested that the kids find a seat and he would place the order. Charlotte's dad always seemed to save the day.

"So, Dillon ... dull party?" Mr. Ramsey asked as he handed the usually talkative boy a double scoop butterscotch special with almonds and rainbow sprinkles.

Maeve looked at Charlotte, who looked around the table. It was her dad. She would have to do the talking. "Julie's brother came in, and we think he and his friends were drinking," Charlotte blurted. "They started making fun of everyone, including Riley, who was there with his band."

"Things got a little out of hand ... did they?" Mr. Ramsey was very matter of fact, for which Charlotte was relieved. It would have been just awful to get a lecture now.

"I hope Julie's party wasn't totally ruined. She looked so sad when people started to leave." Charlotte couldn't stop thinking about the whole thing.

"Julie really looked forward to having a great birthday," Nick agreed, "and the Fabers spent a lot of money to help her celebrate."

"You OK, Katani?" Mr. Ramsey asked.

"Sure. I—it was just kind of crazy there." She looked over at Pete, who nodded in agreement.

"We can get home from here, Mr. Ramsey," Nick said. "Thanks for the ride. I'll call you tomorrow, Charlotte."

Charlotte smiled. Nick said he'd call, right in front of everyone. Dillon got up and left with Nick. Charlotte noticed he didn't tell Maeve good-bye or that he'd call her. She hoped he wasn't mad at Maeve. Maybe his eye was starting to hurt. Pete took one last bite of his sundae, scraped his dish, then left as well.

Katani seemed really tired. Charlotte looked over at her dad. His face had an expression she hadn't seen before. She wondered if he could wait for her to tell him in the morning. All she wanted to do was go home and crawl into bed. The party of the year had turned out to be the biggest bust of the century.

SISTERLY ADVICE

Katani looked at her watch when she got to her room. Kelley was sound asleep. Using the computer wouldn't disturb her. And Katani knew her oldest sister would still be wide awake. Did anyone in college get any sleep? She needed to talk to Candice, immediately.

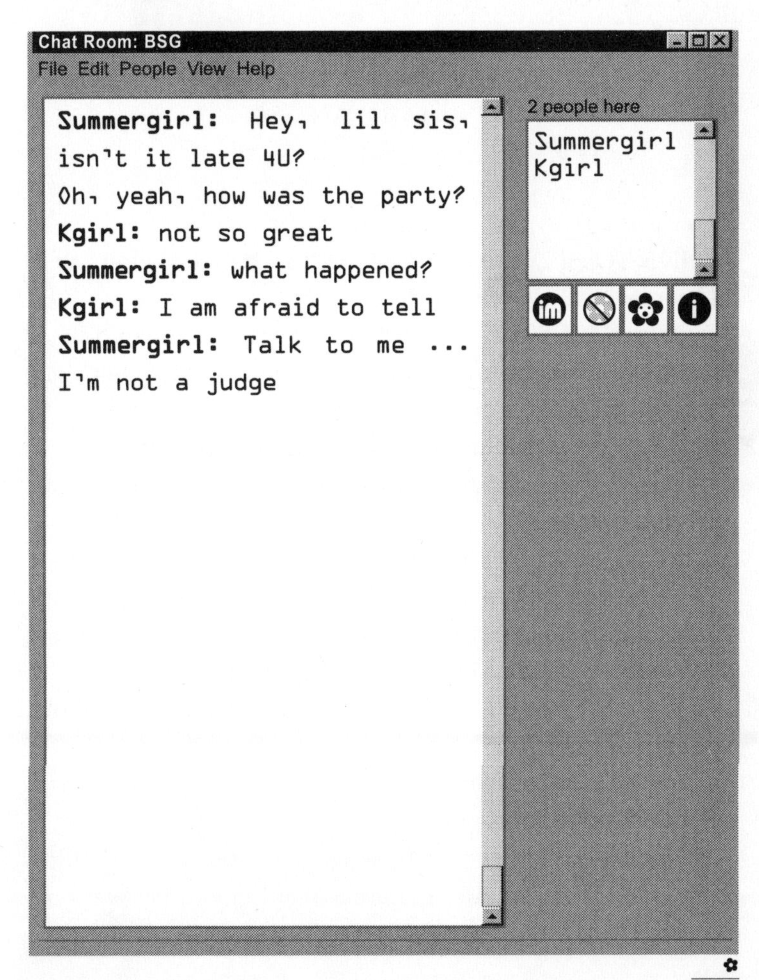

CHAPTER 18

AMBUSH

JOLINE TOSSED things in her locker helter-skelter, as if desperate to find homework.

"I can't believe Tim Cole threw up right in the middle of the floor. It was so gross. And then DJ punched Dillon right in the eye ..."

"Wow, sounds like some party," Robert Worley said.

"Too bad you weren't invited," Anna reminded him. Robert flushed and quickly walked away.

"What a dweeb," Joline grimaced.

"Julie's party was so entertaining. Yeah, if only Katani hadn't ..." Joline stopped in mid sentence. "There she is," Joline said in a very loud voice, just short of shouting.

All heads turned. The Anna and Joline Show was about to begin.

The Queens of Mean spread their witch capes wide and swooped toward their victims.

"Whoa, duck for cover, Katani!" a bemused Avery yelled to her friend, as she put her hands over her head to ward off the evil twins.

Eager classmates surrounded the BSG. Nobody wanted to miss the show. And everyone who hadn't been invited to Julie Faber's party was hoping the BSG would take Anna and Joline down a peg or two or three!

"Two minutes to the bell," Robert Worley called out. Still smarting from Anna's remark, he was trying to show the Queens of Mean that he was still an important part of the group ... Revenge of the Excluded.

Charlotte, Avery, and Maeve looked at Katani, but they stepped close to support her. "What's going on Katani?" Charlotte whispered.

"Ms. BSG Tattletale here," Anna swung her head back and forth and waved her finger in the air, "told Julie Faber's parents that there was drinking and fighting and the whole party was out of control. So the parents came down and kicked everyone out ... just when it was getting good."

"Was that after they cleaned up Tim Cole's throw-up?" Maeve asked ever so sweetly.

Joline shot her the Queen of Mean special look—the one that said, "Back away, lowly insect."

Maeve shrugged and rolled her eyes. Joline Kaminsky didn't scare her.

"You are such a tattletale, Katani. What were you thinking? It's like kindergarten all over again. And Julie is broken hearted," said Kiki Underwood who seemed thrilled to stick her two cents in. "She made herself sick crying. She couldn't even come to school. And her brother can't leave the house for a whole month. Their parents really freaked out. Julie and Bobby both hate you. You think you're so cool, Katani, but you are so immature."

"I ... it was the right thing to do," Katani spoke quietly.

"I hope you're proud of yourself, Miss Party Spoiler," Kiki

said. "Tim and Bobby only drank three beers. It was no biggie."

"That was three too many," Pete Wexler said in Katani's defense. "Those guys were really rude. And what they did was illegal. The Fabers could have been arrested."

"What about Bobby?" Henry asked. "He's the one that broke up Julie's party, not Katani or Julie's parents. My parents would have done the same thing." To Katani's surprise, the Yurtmeister seemed to be on her side.

Anna glared at him. "I thought you were on our side."

"Why do we have to take sides about this?" Charlotte said.

"Ten seconds to the bell," Robert alerted everyone.

"We know whose side you're on. The goody two shoes side. Give me a break. You're all immature babies." Joline slammed her locker and flounced away.

Avery, Maeve, and Charlotte gave each other sidelong glances. They were startled by what had Katani done.

Dillon put his arm around Katani. "The Queens of Mean are riding their brooms today." Then he escorted her to homeroom, leading the way through the crowd who had gathered. Katani heard a few boos and cat calls before she slipped into class.

Ms. Rodriguez stood at the door and greeted her students. She stepped back to let Dillon, Katani, and the BSG in behind her. Isabel had caught up to the crowd in the hall soon enough to hear some of the commotion.

"What happened out there in the hall just now?" a concerned Isabel whispered.

"Tell you later," Avery said. Avery and Isabel knew some of the party details, since they had been IM-ing on Sunday. But neither had heard anything about Katani telling Julie's parents that the party was out of control.

"Good morning, Dillon." Ms. R smiled. "Did you have a

good weekend?"

Dillon grinned at Ms. R. "Sort of. But, you should see the other guy."

It was the standard answer to the age-old question, but Dillon knew the other guy didn't get a scratch, while his eye was going to be black and blue for at least a week.

Dillon shrugged and took his seat.

"I have to admit," Avery said, "I'm sorry that I missed this party after all."

"I think being on TV was probably a better deal," a sarcastic Katani replied.

The BSG hadn't been able to get together on Sunday, but they had chatted online, and Avery had talked to Katani twice on the phone. Not once had Katani mentioned to them that she had gone to Julie's parents about the trouble in the basement.

All eyes went to the front of the classroom where Ms. Rodriguez stood waiting for everyone's attention. She looked especially pretty today in her crisp white shirt and jean skirt. Maeve couldn't help but think that it would be so much fun to be Ms. Rodriguez's matchmaker.

Maeve figured that since she was going to be single herself for about a hundred years, she might as well get a job. Both Riley and Dillon were probably really mad at her, and Tim Cole had three strikes against him—too old, totally inappropriate, and an overall dud. She snuck a look at Dillon. His black and blue and purple and green eye looked terrible. She hoped it didn't hurt. It probably looked worse than it was, but it made her feel awful anyway. But, she thought, as she twirled her hair into a ponytail, how could she have known what would happen? All she wanted to do was dance with Tim Cole. How was that a bad thing to do? Maeve questioned.

✿

"OK, now what was all the uproar about?" Ms. R asked. "Katani, you seem to be the center of attention."

Katani took a deep breath, thought about what Candice had said, and spoke. "Julie Faber's brother and some of his friends came in and caused trouble at Julie's birthday party. They had been drinking and they started a big fight. Tim Cole threw up all over the floor. Some of us decided to leave."

"Wise choice if you ask me," said Ms. R, focusing her attention firmly on Katani.

"Anyway," Katani stuck her chin up. "I decided that Mr. and Mrs. Faber needed to know what was going on. So I told them. If that makes me a tattletale, fine. I don't care what anyone else thinks."

"I don't think it was your place to go and tell the parents, Katani," Dirk Petersen said. "It was none of your business. You ruined the party for everyone else."

"Things weren't that out of control," Patrick Hawk said. "People would have settled down."

"Yeah," Joline put in her two cents. "It wasn't your place to interfere. Julie could have told her parents if she'd wanted them to know. You squealed, Katani. Own up to it."

"OK." Ms. R thought for a moment. "Since this has now become a school issue, let's hear from some of the rest of the class. That OK with you, Katani?" Katani nodded even though she was feeling a little nervous. "Do you think Katani did the right thing … telling Julie's parents?"

"Are you kidding me? Definitely not," Joline insisted.

Lucy Kim raised her hand. "It was Julie's party—she should have taken control of the situation."

"I don't know if she could," Charlotte said. "It seemed to me that Julie didn't know what to do."

"I think there's a difference in reporting something and

being a major tattletale," Riley Lee said. "I was there. The party was out of control big time."

"It was a middle-school party and kids were drinking. That's not cool," Pete Wexler said firmly.

"OK, what's the difference in tattling and reporting?" Ms. R let the question sink in and waited for opinions.

Betsy Fitzgerald waved her hand. "I wasn't at the party, but I think that reporting is telling something that needs to be told. And tattling suggests, well, spite, or meanness. Since Katani had been invited to the party, unlike others in this class who weren't, she wasn't alerting the Fabers out of spite. Maybe she thought someone could get hurt."

"Someone had already gotten hurt." Katani looked over at Dillon.

Murmurs from the class seemed to suggest that Betsy had it right. There was a difference in reporting and tattling.

"So, let me get this straight," Billy Trentini said. "Like, if Avery saw someone breaking into my locker and reported it, she wouldn't be a tattletale?"

"If someone broke into your locker, Billy," Avery said, "no one would have to report it. He'd be lying there on the floor, passed out from the smell."

"Ewwww, dead socks," Sammy said, holding his nose, adding to the laugh that Avery got.

"I think Katani did what she felt was right," Dillon said when the laughter died down. "It was a hard thing to do—she must have known that she was going to make some people mad. But I think she made the right decision."

"Me, too," came from several voices. Katani kept her head down, doodling on a page in her notebook. She was glad for Betsy's speech. She was glad Ms. R had given them a chance to talk about the situation. To be thought of as a tattletale by her whole class would have been more than she could handle. Candice had emailed her grandmother, telling her there might be a problem at school on Monday. But Katani had a talk with Grandma Ruby and asked her not to make this into a big school thing. It was hard enough for Katani to live a normal life when her grandmother was principal of Abigail Adams Junior High.

"All right, class. We're going to start today's class off with some free writing. I want you to take out pen and paper and write on the subject of personal responsibility in the face of a potentially dangerous situation." There were groans. Some kids hated free writing. They felt it was pointless.

Ms. R paused. "Remember, with free writing, you just write anything that comes to your mind. It doesn't even have to make sense at the time. You're tapping into your subconscious mind."

"What if there's nothing in my subconscious mind?" Dillon asked. He was one of the students that loved this type of assignment. It meant he didn't have to watch his spelling or grammar. To Dillon, free writing was a great deal.

"From what I have overheard, Dillon, I'd think there'd be a little bit there today." Ms. R smiled back at him.

"Don't look around for inspiration. Just start writing and continue until I say time is up."

The class got even quieter than usual. Apparently there was a lot on people's minds today. Or they just kept writing the same word over and over as Ms. R said they could do in this exercise.

"Time," Ms. R said finally, although she usually didn't let them write for more than ten minutes, and more often it was five. "As you know, writings like this are private, but would anyone like to share?"

Betsy Fitzgerald waved her hand. Here we go again, Avery thought. Betsy to the rescue. What else was new?

"All right, Betsy." Ms. R sat on a high stool by her desk.

Betsy cleared her throat. "Responsibility is when you may be only one person, but one person can make a difference. Sometimes it takes guts to do what you think is right, like Katani did. However, if you're part of a team, you're responsible to everyone on the team. Like in basketball, if you don't practice, and it happens to be you who has the chance to score the winning point right before the buzzer, and you miss, then you've let your team down. So there's individual responsibility and team responsibility. Your team should let you have the chance to score sometimes, even when you don't have a lot of experience."

Avery looked at Isabel, shrugged and grinned.

"I wonder if you're thinking about today's basketball game, Betsy? By the way, congratulations on making the team. I didn't know you played basketball."

"I didn't. But I realized when you fill out college applications, they are looking for well-rounded people. I decided I wasn't very well rounded."

Little laughs escaped all over the room.

Billy Trentini lay back in his chair, shaking his head. Betsy drove him crazy with all her college talk.

"That's right. Colleges look at more than grades when they choose their new freshmen. Good luck today, Betsy, and all the rest of the team." Ms. R looked at Avery.

Avery didn't take the cue to read. Maeve shook her head and Charlotte pretended that she was looking in her notebook. None of the BSG wanted to comment any more on Katani's decision in front of the whole class. They were glad that some other people outside their group had defended

Katani. It seemed like a real blow to the Queens of Mean, who were trying to paint Katani as a major tattletale.

❧

At lunch, the Beacon Street Girls finally got a chance to talk more about the party.

"So Katani, what made you tell the Fabers?"

Katani stared at her food before answering. "I just really thought that 12 and 13 year olds shouldn't be involved with drinking. I mean, what if something happened to Tim Cole? What if he passed out and didn't wake up? That kind of stuff happens a lot. I've heard about it from my older sisters."

"That was brave, Katani. As the Aussies say, *Good on you*," Charlotte said.

Avery piped in, "That was hard to do. I think it's awesome that you stood up for what you thought was right, knowing that other kids might make fun of you for it."

The other girls nodded in support. Katani almost cried. To have such good friends like the BSG was the best thing about being in seventh grade at Abigail Adams Junior High.

"I wish that I had never gone to that party," Maeve looked depressed.

"It wasn't like you were actually responsible for the fighting, Maeve," Katani said. "Bobby started it by bringing his friends to the party when Julie had asked him to stay away. In fact, Mr. and Mrs. Faber should have made sure Bobby had something else to do."

"But the fight was about me. I should have gone with you when you asked." Maeve toyed with her lunch, dipping a carrot stick into spaghetti sauce.

"The drinking was Bobby's fault, too," Isabel said. "My sister says he looks for ways to cause trouble."

"So let me get this straight," Avery said. "Riley came to Maeve's defense with DJ. DJ meant to hit Riley, but Dillon stepped in at just that moment, so DJ hit Dillon."

"I didn't ask them to help me. Honest I didn't. I would have been all right. I feel so bad for Dillon. He's the one with the black eye."

"He's getting lots of attention because of it," Avery said. "Dillon loves attention. But maybe you should say sorry, Maeve. It can't hurt."

"Do you think I should write up the party for the school newspaper?" asked Charlotte.

"No way! It wasn't a school thing, and not everyone was invited." Maeve looked at Charlotte. "Besides, it's old news. Everyone in the school knows what happened by now." Maeve giggled. "It is kind of romantic, though. Remember that movie called *Sabrina* where they had a big fight at the end? Both brothers liked Audrey Hepburn. One was a serious businessman and the other a playboy."

"Leave it to Maeve to turn all this into a movie. But personally, if someone threw up right in front of me, I wouldn't be thinking any romantic thoughts." Avery finished up her lunch, blew up her paper lunch bag, and popped it. Then she hid it immediately, since such behavior was frowned on in the cafeteria.

"I feel like that paper bag," Avery said. "I'm about to pop. How many are coming to the game to watch Isabel and me score all the points, except for the last, winning basket, of course? We'll give the ball to Betsy, she'll cause someone to foul her, get a free throw, and she'll be the heroine." Avery acted out the scenario as she made up the story.

"We're all coming, Ave," Charlotte said. "We wouldn't miss it for the world. Then we'll go straight to the Tower to finish this discussion. Dad said he'd have pizzas by 6:00.

"Char?" Maeve asked. "We haven't talked nearly enough about your poem, and Riley turning it into a song. That was so cool."

"Yes, it was unbelievable." Charlotte got a dreamy look on her face.

Maeve picked up her lunch tray and hurried ahead of them to turn it in and go to afternoon classes. "Play your heart out, Ave. You too, Isabel."

"Be there or be trapezoid." Avery bounced an imaginary basketball all the way back to class. Occasionally, she tossed the ball to Isabel, who tossed it back. Charlotte and Katani were their designated cheerleaders.

By the time they got to the locker area, Maeve had disappeared.

"Do you think Maeve's all right?" Charlotte said.

"Oh, she is. Maybe she went on to class with Dillon."

CHAPTER 19

POINTS FOR ALL

"IT'S JUST TOO hard to get back in the swing of things today," Charlotte complained.

"When I am the CEO of Kgirl Enterprises, we'll go to three-day weekends," Katani said. "Monday will be set aside for recovering from Saturday and Sunday."

"Absolutely smashing idea." Charlotte mulled over what books to take home for their study session that night in the Tower. Math ... she suddenly remembered that they still needed to help Maeve with math.

"But first things first," Katani said. "Isabel and Avery got out fifteen minutes early to suit up for the game, but where's Maeve?"

"I don't know. She disappeared after last class." Charlotte felt a little bit worried, but Maeve knew they were going to the game.

"We'd better go on. I have to take Kelley." Katani looked up and down the hall.

"Hi, Charlotte," Kelley said when Ruby Fields delivered her to her sister's locker. "Are you going to the basketball game? It's going to be supercalifragilistic fun. I love basketball. It's so round." Kelley began jumping about like one of the dancing hippos in *Fantasia*.

Katani leaned her head against her locker. "Grandma Ruby, I don't ..."

"We're all going together, Kelley." Charlotte hooked her arm into Kelley's and started walking down the hallway. "Come on. We'll come back for books later."

A relieved Katani gave her grandma a quick hug and traipsed after her sister and Charlotte.

"You're my best friend in the whole world, Charlotte," Kelley said. "I liked you since the first day of school, didn't I?"

"Yes you did. Despite it being the disaster of all time." Charlotte smiled.

"Today was a big disaster," Kelley said. "I spilled my milk all over Denash at lunch and then I couldn't do my work."

Katani looked at Charlotte. "I hope you're finished with spilling things today, Kelley," Katani said as she rolled her eyes at Charlotte.

"Oh, yeah, it was just one of those crazy unfortunate things. Unfortunate." Kelley had obviously fallen in love with a new word. "Unfortunate! Unfortunate!" She repeated it all the way to the gym.

Charlotte, Katani, and Kelley got seats in the middle, three bleachers up so they could see really well.

"I'll save a seat for Maeve with my jacket." Charlotte placed her favorite vintage blue jean jacket across the bleacher beside her.

"Where's Maeve?" Kelley asked. "I like that red-haired girl. She's sparkly." Charlotte chuckled. Kelley was so on target sometimes.

"It's a mystery," Katani said, "unless she's secretly

practicing with Riley's band again. Now hush, Kelley, and get ready to watch and cheer for Avery and Isabel."

"Yea, Avery! Yea, Isabel!" Kelley shouted, and then she waved when Avery and Isabel stopped their warmup practice to wave back.

"Sit down, Kelley," Katani hissed. It was just so embarrassing to be with Kelley sometimes. Katani wished that she had her favorite hoodie on right now so she could hide her head. Maybe it was the whole tattletale incident, but she had had enough embarrassment for one day. Kelley sat down, crossed her arms, and stuck her face up to Katani's.

"Miss Cranky Crank," she called her sister and then turned back to watch the game.

So Sorry

Maeve had left last period science class with Avery, Isabel, and several cheerleaders, hoping Mr. Moore wouldn't know who was supposed to leave and who wasn't. Whatever. There were only fifteen minutes left.

Slipping out the school's back door, she pulled on her jacket, sat on the steps, and pulled out the letter she'd found stuck in the vents of her locker after lunch. She had read it once, quickly, but wanted to read it again.

Dear Maeve,

I am really sorry (I mean really, really sorry) about what happened at Julie's party. I don't know what got into me. Well, I do know. It was beer, 3 beers. I'm not used to drinking and I also ate too much pizza (you probably figured that out already.) I hope I didn't mess up your jeans too badly. I hope you don't think I drink all the time, since I don't. In fact that was the first time ever.

✿

Bobby dared me to chug a whole beer before we came to the party. It was a huge mistake on my part. If I'd known how it would make me act, I'd have said no. I do like you and you are a great dance partner.

I'll apologize to Dillon in a couple of days. I probably won't write him a letter, though, 'cause guys think that kind of stuff is weird. You may never want to see me or talk to me again, but if you do, meet me behind the school after last class for just a couple of minutes.

If you aren't there, I'll understand.

Your friend, and dance partner I hope,

Tim

P.S. My mother did not make me write this letter.

Maeve thought it was pretty brave of Tim to write her a letter. And to want to see her to apologize. She didn't know if they could be friends, but she would talk to him.

Where was he? She looked at her pink Minnie Mouse watch. She didn't want to miss any of the basketball game. And Charlotte and Katani would wonder where she was.

"Maeve?" Tim had walked up behind Maeve without her hearing.

She swung around, stuffing the letter in her purse. "Thanks for writing me this letter."

"I didn't know what else to do. I was afraid you wouldn't speak to me again."

"I wasn't sure either. But, it was a nice letter. It's just that I didn't like how you acted at the party. I don't like being around boys who drink and throw up on my pants. I did like dancing with you in our hip hop class." Maeve was rarely at a loss for words, but she didn't know what else to say to Tim.

"Will you dance with me next class?"

"I don't know." Maeve got up. "I have to go. I promised my friends I'd watch their basketball game."

"I was going to the game too. Can I walk you there?"

"Ah ... They're saving me a seat. See you later." Maeve practically ran back in the school, down the hall to the gym, to get ahead of Tim. Walking into the gym with him would finish off the disaster of the weekend. Shouting and cheering spilled over into the hall, so she knew she was late.

She hurried inside, looked around, and finally spotted Kelley waving at her. "'Scuse me, 'scuse me." She made her way down the row.

"Maeve!" Kelley yelled over the crowd. "Where were you? The BSG were soooo upset. But, we saved you a seat." Katani rolled her eyes at Maeve. Kelley was so full of herself today.

Maeve sat down quickly. She had already called enough attention to herself this week. "Thanks, Kelley. What's the score?"

"16 to 14. Very unfortunate." Kelley took Maeve's hand. "I'm glad you're here. You're one of my very best friends. I like your red hair."

Maeve didn't know why, but Kelley's declaration of friendship was very reassuring. She needed her friends right now. Maybe she was feeling a little afraid that like in Charlotte's poem, if she wasn't careful, they could all wash right out from under her feet like sand when the tide goes out, and she'd be left alone. No friends? Life without the BSG was a disaster she couldn't even imagine.

Suddenly, the crowd surged to their feet, wildly cheering. Avery sunk a jump shot from the top of the key.

"Yea, Avery!" Maeve shouted. The BSG all clapped for their friend.

The opposing team, Lincoln, inbounded the ball to a girl

wearing number 23, and she started to dribble up the court. Since Avery was playing point guard, she guarded no. 23 as the girl dribbled the length of the floor. After they crossed midcourt, no. 23 spotted an open teammate and tried to pass the ball to her, but Avery was too quick. She reached out just in time to block the pass, steal the ball, and sprint toward the other basket.

Julie and Anna also took off, and it was three on one going down the court. Avery passed to Anna, who passed to Julie, who laid it up and in off the backboard. Abigail Adams 24, Lincoln 22. Avery and Julie high-fived as they ran back to play defense.

"Whoa, looks like Avery and Julie are getting along now," observed Maeve.

"Well, in order to play as a team, you have to put all your differences aside," explained Charlotte. "Remember, there's no 'I' in TEAM!"

The buzzer sounded at the end of the half and both teams jogged to their benches for the halftime break.

"Alright, we're going to start off the second half with the veterans," Coach Porter announced. "Kayla, you'll be at center. Jenny and Amanda at forward, and Sarah and Min at guard. You guys are playing great! Let's keep it up in the second half!"

Avery sat back on the bench and drank from her water bottle. She hated to sit on the bench, but everybody had to get a chance to play. She was having a ton of fun so far, and Julie and company were actually working with their teammates instead of sabotaging the team with their meanness. Julie must still feel bad after her party, figured Avery.

The score stayed close throughout the second half. Coach Porter subbed the players in and out and made sure that everyone got to play.

Up in the stands, the girls were having a great time cheering on the Abigail Adams team.

"Go Avery!" Kelley shouted.

"Go Isabel!" Charlotte called out.

"Go Betsy, go!" Katani shook her head. "She is unbelievable today."

"Go Anna!" Maeve finally got into the game. She started yelling for everyone. Yelling made her feel a whole lot better. Maybe someday she could teach yelling therapy. Maybe she would be a yelling therapist when she grew up. She could see her card now, "Maeve Kaplan-Taylor—Yelling Therapist to the Stars." Her tagline would read: *Shout Your Blues Away*. Of course, her card would be pink. Pink would always be her signature color. Ms. Razzberry Pink told her that anyone who chose pink as their signature color would always be able to beat the blues.

✿

The clock was winding down in the fourth quarter and Abigail Adams was still down by two points. A Lincoln player took a shot and missed, and Isabel pulled down the rebound.

"Time out, ref!" called Coach Porter.

The teams huddled around their coaches at their respective benches.

"Alright, Avery, you're going in for Sarah. Betsy, you're in for Isabel. Anna, Amanda, and Jenny, you'll all stay in. We've got twenty seconds left in the game and we need two to tie." Coach Porter took out her clipboard and a marker and started to draw a play on the surface. "We're going to run play number five. Jenny, you'll inbound the ball to Avery, and Amanda, you'll cut toward the open space. Avery, your job is to get the ball to Amanda when she's open. Amanda, if you get a good look, take the shot. Everybody got it?"

All the players nodded.

"OK, everybody in," Coach said, placing her hand in the center of the tight circle. The whole team put their hands in for a cheer. "Team on three. 1, 2, 3 ..."

"TEAM!" they all shouted as they shook their hands in unison.

Up in the stands, the other BSG watched Avery run out on the court and get in position.

"Oh, I'm so nervous for Avery!" said Maeve.

"Don't worry, Maeve," Katani said. "Avery totally thrives on pressure!"

Jenny Pesky inbounded the ball to Avery and she dribbled to the right, looking for the open player. Amanda ran under the basket and cut to the left, trying to lose her defender. Avery got ready to pass, but suddenly Amanda tripped and fell to the court. There was no foul, so the refs didn't blow the whistle. *Oh no!* thought Avery. *Now I can't pass to Amanda!*

Avery glanced at the game clock. Only ten seconds left. She kept dribbling and saw Betsy open at the top of the key. Avery passed the ball to Betsy, who dribbled toward the hoop. Betsy's going to do a lay up, thought Avery. Betsy's defender whacked her on the arm just as she was letting go of the ball, and the buzzer sounded. The referee blew the whistle, and the ball bounced off the backboard and hit the rim, bounced back above the basket and fell straight through the hoop. The score was tied! And Betsy was fouled, so she would get to take one foul shot.

If Betsy hit her foul shot, Abigail Adams would win. Luckily for Abigail Adams, Betsy was the best free throw shooter on the team. The gym was silent as Betsy took her time bouncing the basketball a couple of times at the foul line. She lined up her shot, just like she practiced every day. Betsy bent her knees and extended her arm and shot the ball. Time seemed to slow down as the ball arched toward the basket. Swish! Nothing but net. The crowd went wild.

"Yeah!" cheered Avery as she high-fived Betsy. "You did it, Betsy!"

The Abigail Adams players rushed onto the court to congratulate Betsy, clapping and high-fiving. By working together, and playing their best, they had won the game.

After shaking hands with Lincoln, Isabel and Avery ran to the stands to see their friends.

"We won!" Avery shouted, hugging Kelley. "Did you see that, Kelley? We won our first game. And half of us were new to the team."

"How unfortunate for the other team that you are so great," answered a very serious Kelley.

Avery hugged Kelley and turned to Charlotte.

"You were outstanding too, Isabel," Charlotte said.

"Adams had the best team strategy. Where'd you learn to shoot like that, Isabel?"

"I've been practicing and Avery has helped me a lot. I just didn't know if I could play under pressure. Did you see what Betsy was doing?"

"We saw it. I guess genius is good for more than college applications." Charlotte laughed as she gathered up her things.

"You're my best basketball friends, Avery and Isabel," Kelley said, holding hands with both of them as they walked to the showers.

"Come on, Kelley," Katani said. "Grandma Ruby will be waiting for us. And Avery and Isabel have to shower."

Kelley stretched her arms in the air. "I would like to shower too. It smells in that unfortunate gym."

Katani couldn't help herself. She laughed hard at that one.

Kelley gave her a hug. "Happy day. Ms. Cranky Crank is now Ms. Sweetie Pie."

CHAPTER 20

AFTERMATH

"DO YOU REALLY have to take the math test again?" Avery asked Maeve as the BSG walked up Corey Hill toward Charlotte's house.

"Yeah. I really do. But first my parents and I are going to meet with the Crow and Mrs. Fields. We are all going to sit around and discuss the 'Maeve math problem.'"

"I think I would rather eat worms," grimaced Isabel. Avery picked up a piece of grass and dangled it in front of Isabel's face. Isabel swatted Avery's hand away with a giggle.

Joining in on the fun, Maeve raised her eyebrows in a perfect imitation of her dear math teacher. "If only Ms. Taylor-Kaplan would pay attention, do her homework, listen to my fabulous equations and follow my incredible problem sets, then everything would be perfect, and Ms. Taylor-Kaplan would be my best C student."

The girls broke up. Maeve was such an incredible mimic. Charlotte thought her friend would be great at cartoon voices.

"Seriously, Maeve. I heard a group talking in the girls' room about the test. You aren't the only one who flunked. I think you should bring that up at the meeting. Maybe they could start a special math support group or something," Charlotte said as she adjusted her backpack. She was carrying way too many books. She didn't care how dweebish a rolling backpack was, she was going to ask her father for one for Christmas.

"A math support group is the coolest idea," Katani exclaimed.

Maeve's face took on a devilish look. "We could do relaxation exercises." She flung Avery on the grass and stood over her waving a fake magic wand. "Repeat after me. You are not afraid of math. Math is your friend. Math is tasty and delicious, and will help you grow up to be big and strong and very crow like."

That did it. Charlotte and Isabel fell on the grass laughing so hard a woman yelled out of an apartment window to see if they were all right.

"Get up, you goofballs," Katani ordered, "before they call the paramedics."

The girls flew toward Charlotte's house to find that Marty had heard them from a block or so away. He was flinging himself against the door as Charlotte stuck her key in. When he saw Avery, he yipped and yapped and danced until she scooped him up.

"Ready to go to the hospital, Marty? Dress like a clown, do tricks, or maybe you can wear your Klondike Marty outfit if Maeve will give up her slipper again."

"Promise me, Avery," Isabel sounded serious, "you won't dress him like a clown. I hate clowns, too. Dress him in a tux like in the magic show. He looked very handsome, didn't you, Marty?" Marty cocked his head back and forth as Isabel spoke. When she was finished, Marty yelped in agreement. No clown costumes for the little dude.

"OK, but I am taking Marty to pet therapy school," Avery replied. She tickled the little guy under his chin.

"I like how the little dude always knows we're coming," Charlotte said.

Avery agreed. "Yeah, I think that's why he would make a great pet therapy dog." Katani led the way to Charlotte's bedroom while Charlotte went to let her father know they were home.

After unloading their books, all five BSG headed back downstairs to the kitchen where Mr. Ramsey had opened five pizzas. The delicious smell of cheese, tomato, pepperoni, and spices filled the air.

"I anticipated that you girls might need a little study fuel," Mr. Ramsey said. "We've got plain cheese, we've got a pepperoni, we've got a mushroom and onion …"

"I think I'll pass on the pepperoni," Maeve said with a faint smile. The vision of red punch and pepperoni chunks spewing out of Tim Cole's mouth wasn't one that she would soon forget.

"We better finish up because I have to leave 'precisely at 9 o'clock.'" Katani imitated her father's stern tone.

"Ditto," said Maeve and Avery together.

"One of our parents will drop you off, Isabel," Avery said.

The girls climbed the stairs to the Tower room. Every time they entered the Tower, they felt a shiver of excitement. The Tower was their special place, a room of their own to be themselves: dreamy, klutzy Charlotte; quirky, artistic Isabel; sparkly, bad-at-math Maeve; sporty, opinionated Avery; stylish, reserved Katani. A place for friends to figure out how to grow up loyal and true. It also happened to be an awesomely cool room with windows to see all of Boston, and each girl had her own favorite spot, uniquely decorated to fit her personality.

✿

Katani went directly for her great-grandfather's Lime Swivel—the barber's chair that he used to cut Jackie Kennedy style bobs from years ago.

Avery, who was the president of BSG, took charge.

"OK, I call the BSG to order. And BSG, we're going to have to stay totally focused in order to have time for studying."

Everyone groaned and chorused, "Do we have to?"

"We said we were coming here to study," Avery reminded them.

"Sometimes we have to play first." Maeve jumped up. "You gotta check out this move." She proceeded to demonstrate her newest dance. Katani, Charlotte, and Isabel went crazy when Avery attempted to imitate her.

Finally, Katani sat, folding her legs yoga style, and waited for Maeve to settle down.

"OK. First up … Maeve. Inquiring minds want to know, why were you late to the basketball game?"

"Is there time for personal reports?" Maeve asked Avery.

"I guess so. I have something to report myself." Avery sat down. "You first, Maeve. Why were you late to the most important *first* girls' basketball game of the year?"

"I was with Tim Cole." Maeve let the astonishment sink in, then she hurried to say, "Only for a minute. When I went back to my locker at noon, he had left me a note. And he asked me to meet him after school."

"What did he have to say about the way he behaved at the party?" Avery asked, looking at the note Maeve shared.

"He apologized. He asked me to forgive him, and then when we met in person, he asked me to dance with him in hip hop class."

"He should have apologized. He was very rude to throw up on you." Isabel held Marty, who was quite content to be adored by one of his BSG.

"I know. I probably will forgive him, 'cause I don't want to be one of those people who holds a grudge forever and ever," Maeve said.

"Yeah, a weekend is forever," Katani commented with a wry smile.

"Very funny, Ms. Cranky Crank," chuckled Maeve. "Truth or dare, though, I don't like him as much anymore. He's cute and everything, but if somebody can dare him to do something stupid like chug a beer, he's not my kind of guy. But dancing with him is another thing."

"So you'll go back to Dillon for your main crush?" Charlotte uncapped her water bottle and took a big swallow.

"I'm so done with crushes. Boys are fun to be with, but I've resolved not to obsess so much over boys and obsess more over math."

Avery took out her chart. "Let's give Maeve an A+ for having a healthy dose of common sense."

Maeve stood up and bowed. "My first A+." All the BSG clapped enthusiastically, even Maeve.

"Charlotte?" Isabel asked. "You look like you have something to say."

"Well, Tim really didn't show respect at all for Julie Faber when he was drinking, crashed the party, then expected a guest to dance with him."

Katani nodded. "Girls need to always be sure guys treat us with respect."

"Katani and Charlotte receive As for their thoughtful remarks." Avery nodded.

"Hey, how come we don't get A+ like Maeve?" Katani's competitive spirit was kicking in.

"Because," Avery spoke in a tone usually reserved for

the third graders she coached in soccer, "Tim Cole did not throw up on you." Katani threw a pillow at Avery's head.

"Seriously, I think it's a girl's job to know her boundaries. My mother always says that," Maeve explained. "You have to practice saying no. So that if somebody is really pressing you to do something you don't want to do, you feel comfortable telling them to politely buzz off."

"It's like Betsy and her free throws. She practiced and when the time came she was ready to sink that basketball," said Avery.

"I think we should give Betsy an A+ for effort," Katani proposed. "Clap if you agree."

All the BSG clapped loudly and long for Betsy, the nerdy girl, who annoyed everyone every day of her life with her obsessions about achieving the perfect college resume.

"You know, I am going to propose amendment number eleven to The New Tower Rules: 'We will always think before we act,'" Avery noted. "Tim Cole wouldn't be in such major trouble with everyone if he had used a little brain power. What's the vote?"

Katani, Charlotte, and Isabel spoke up quickly in favor of the amendment.

"I hereby resolve I will always think before I act," Maeve held up her hand and swore.

Everyone laughed, wondering how long Maeve's resolution would last. Like New Year's resolutions, maybe a week. Life with Maeve was so entertaining and never predictable, Charlotte thought.

"Charlotte, do you have anything to say? After all, you were a star at the party. Do you think Riley will make his own CD soon? It's pretty cheap to do that. And he could sell them for less than CDs of famous bands in stores."

"I'm sure he's thought of that," Charlotte said. "I gave him that poem a long time ago and thought he had thrown it out. Or that he didn't like it or think the poem would set to music."

"So maybe you'll become a songwriter instead of an author and poet?" Katani asked.

"Why can't I do all of those things when I grow up? *No limits* is my new motto."

"I would like to make a special award for this evening," Katani announced.

"Go for it, Kgirl." Avery handed her friend the BSG official meeting notes.

"I nominate Isabel and Avery for the BSG humanitarian award for being super volunteers for kids with cancer."

Isabel put her hands to her face and Avery put a pillow over her head as Charlotte, Katani, and Maeve thumped, whistled, and clapped for their BSG buddies.

"You can come with us to the hospital if you like. They have a pet visitation program. I want us to train Marty even better, teach him more tricks, and take him in to visit the kids. That's my announcement." Avery sounded so excited with the possibility of bringing Marty to visit.

"And Maeve," Isabel piped in, "I bet the kids would love it if you and Riley put a show on there."

"Yeah," Avery jumped up and started pacing. "These kids are just like us except they have to fight cancer. They want to have fun, and eat junk food, and laugh. If we include other girls in some of our projects, we could do a lot of fun stuff for the kids."

"Like math?" Maeve said half seriously. "Maybe if I have to stay in seventh grade and take math over again, it won't be too bad. I can be the most mature person in the class."

"Maeve," a suddenly very mature sounding Katani

explained, "you are not going to have to repeat seventh grade. Mr. Sherman is just going to have to figure something out."

"Besides," said Avery, "We aren't going to let you flunk, even if it takes all of us working weekends and nights to help you pass your tests."

"Speaking of work ..." Charlotte sighed. "I hate to be the nag, but this was supposed to be a study session, and I have one more page to write for my social studies report. Then I have to check it over to make sure it's really finished."

Maeve opened her math book reluctantly.

Charlotte giggled when Maeve lay down and used her book as a pillow. Maybe she thought it would sink into her brain more easily that way.

"Let's plan our twentieth high school reunion now."

Avery whistled through her teeth like she would at a football game. Marty barked and ran in circles to give everyone a face lick. Then he got Happy Lucky Thingy and held it down with his front paws as if it would escape.

"I declare this meeting perfect, and if we can study for one hour, we'll still have some time left to visit. Maeve, it's 7:15. If we study for an hour and ten minutes, how much longer can we visit?"

Maeve looked at Avery. "Be quiet!"

Each girl laughed, scooted off alone, and got to work. Maeve opened her math book and started to work some problems. She looked at her watch, gave herself ten minutes per problem, which was Matt's new suggestion for desensitizing her anxiety about working under pressure. Avery started reading a new book for English class. Isabel sketched some ideas for cartoons for the next issue of *The Sentinel*. Katani was designing a cover for her social studies report. Charlotte finished her paper quickly, then decided to write an article for the paper about friendship.

It was 8 o'clock when Charlotte heard the doorbell ring, then her father called to them.

"Girls, can you take a break? There are some people here that I think you'd like to speak to."

Who would be at Charlotte's door, wanting to see any of them? They slipped on shoes and hurried downstairs.

Mr. Ramsey had closed the door. Charlotte opened it slowly, then swung it wide.

Nick, Dillon, Pete Wexler, and the Trentini twins stood on the doorstep. Dillon grinned and pointed to his bruised eye, now purple, green, and brown. "Trick or Treat," he joked.

Nick smiled at Charlotte, who felt her face heat up. She hoped it was too dark for him to notice.

"It must be time for a break," Billy Trentini said. "Your father said you were studying, but we know better."

"We were studying, Billy," Charlotte said.

"Yeah, I'll bet." Dillon looked at Maeve. "You were studying math all evening."

"Not all evening. We had other things we needed to talk about." Maeve gripped Charlotte's arm so hard that Charlotte almost squealed before she could stop herself.

"Well, I declare recess," Nick grinned. "Time for some fun. How about some games of speed checkers at Montoya's. My dad said he'd keep the shop open for a private party."

"Excuse us, for a minute." Avery shut the door. "We have to vote on this, and all of us have to agree we're through with our work."

"Avery," all the BSG stifled giggles.

"All in favor of taking a speed-checker break, signify by saying yea."

The yeas were unanimous. Mr. Ramsey waved an OK to

Charlotte. Avery opened the door. "We would be honored to accompany you to Montoya's. But we all have to be back here by five minutes of nine. Agreed?"

"No problem," Nick said.

The girls grabbed their jackets and joined the boys to walk down to Beacon Street for a game of speed checkers at Montoya's Bakery.

"This is more fun than the Party of the Year," whispered Charlotte to Nick. Nick reached out for Charlotte's hand.

To: Sophie
From: Charlotte
Subject: Song Writer

Dear Sophie,

You will not believe that I am now officially a song writer. Riley Lee, a boy I hope I have mentioned, who formed a band called Mustard Monkey, took a poem I wrote and set it to music. The song has a verse about Orangina. I will attach the whole poem here. I wish you could have been at the party to hear the song. I miss you. If you have written any more poems, please send. If you have found Orangina or seen her again, please tell me.

Au revoir, Charlotte

To be continued ...

AVAILABLE JUNE '06 AT:

www.beaconstreetgirls.com and
local bookstores everywhere!

lucky charm

Marty is missing! The Beacon Street Girls begin a desperate search for their beloved doggie mascot. To top it off, the local riding stable where Katani and Kelley have recently discovered their love of horses is in danger of closing its doors. Will the Beacon Street Girls be able to make a difficult decision without breaking their friendship apart? Will Marty ever come home to his Beacon Street Girls?

keep up to date with the BSG at beaconstreetgirls.com

freaked out Book Extras

- Book Club Buzz
- Charlotte's Word Nerd Dictionary
- Trivialicious Trivia
- Dr. Knight Speaks About Alcohol

5 Questions for You and Your Friends to Chat About

1. Have you ever been left out? Did you feel the same way as Avery, or did you have different feelings?

2. Have you ever felt panicked because of a big test at school? How did you work through the problem?

3. Do you think Katani did the right thing by telling the Fabers about the out-of-control party?

4. What lessons did Maeve and the rest of the BSG learn from Julie Faber's party?

5. Which characters in *Freaked Out* actually "freaked out"?

more *Freaked Out* Book Club Buzz at beaconstreetgirls.com

Charlotte Ramsey

Charlotte's Word Nerd Dictionary

BSG Words

Romanticking: (p. 95) verb—gushing about someone you have a crush on

Spanish Words & Phrases

Lo Siento: (p. 49) I'm sorry
Equipo: (p. 93) noun—team
Loca: (p. 120) adjective—crazy
Hombre: (p. 120) noun—man
Chico: (p. 121) noun—boy; man
De Nada: (p. 161)—you're welcome

Other Cool Words ...

Snarky: (p. 1) adjective—unfriendly; angry
Akimbo: (p. 2) adjective—bent in different directions
Askance: (p. 10) adverb—suspiciously
Prodigious: (p. 14) adjective—large; impressive
Palindrome: (p. 14) noun—a word or phrase that is spelled

the same backwards and forwards (A Toyota)
Solidarity: (p. 22) noun—sticking together with another person or group
Gobbledygook: (p. 24) noun—a jumble; something that cannot be understood
Testament: (p. 33) noun—proof that something is true
Melodramatic: (p. 41) adjective—really emotional and dramatic
Diabolical: (p. 57) adjective—evil
Impromptu: (p. 75) adjective—spur of the moment; unplanned
Elusive: (p. 84) adjective—out of reach; hard to find or understand
Interlude: (p. 110) noun—a short period of time during which something different happens
Protagonists: (p. 133) noun—main characters in books, plays, movies, or TV shows
Morale: (p. 136) noun—spirit; usually connected to emotional condition in the face of opposition
Detour: (p. 155) noun—a block in the road that sends you in a different direction
Unanimous: (p. 156) adjective—when every person votes "yes"
Crinoline: (p. 166) noun—a stiff piece of fabric; a petticoat

freaked out **trivialicious trivia**

1. Who is "the Crow"?
   A. Ms. Rodriguez
   B. Mr. Sherman
   C. Mr. McCarthy
   D. Mrs. Fields

2. What is Betsy Fitzgerald's latest trick for getting into an Ivy League college?
   A. Studying 24 hours a day
   B. Becoming an Irish step dancing champion
   C. Perfecting her free throws in basketball
   D. Learning every word in the dictionary

3. What is the theme of Julie Faber's party?
   A. 1970s disco
   B. Costume
   C. Red, white, and blue
   D. Hawaiian

4. What color belt does Sam get at his Tae Kwon Do test?
   A. Yellow
   B. Green
   C. Purple
   D. Black

5. What kind of vehicle do the kids from the hospital use to get through the drive thru?
   A. a unicycle
   B. a bicycle
   C. a motorcycle
   D. a You-Can't-Stop-Us Mobile

ANSWERS: 1. B. Mr. Sherman **2. C.** perfecting her free throws in basketball **3. D.** Hawaiian **4. A.** Yellow **5. D.** A You-Can't-Stop-Us Mobile

more *Freaked Out* Trivialicious Trivia at beaconstreetgirls.com

BSG

Be the first to find out about new books, products, contests, and special offers ✿

✿ Share your opinions with other BSG fans

Sign up now and get a free gift
(while supplies last)

Don't forget to visit www.beaconstreetgirls.com. We have games, quizzes, and a BSG shop!

Join Now! totally **FREE!**

www.beaconstreetgirls.com

Dr. John Knight currently serves as an Associate Professor of Pediatrics at Harvard Medical School and as the Director of the Center for Adolescent Substance Abuse Research at Children's Hospital Boston. Dr. Knight conducts scientific studies on the early identification and treatment of alcohol and drug problems in teenagers. He is a fellow of the American Academy of Pediatrics.

M: What exactly is alcohol?

Dr. K: Alcohol is made from fruits and vegetables like grapes and potatoes. When it is processed, the sugar from the fruit or vegetable turns into a chemical called ethyl alcohol or ethanol.

M: Why do people like to drink alcohol?

Dr. K: Alcohol in small amounts can make you feel relaxed and sociable. Some young people experiment with alcohol because drinking makes them feel "cool" and more adult like. However, there is a reason that the drinking age is 21. Alcohol is more dangerous to young people than to adults. It is a drug and if you drink enough you could become addicted. Alcohol can be very dangerous to your health and well being.

M: What is Alcoholism?

Dr. K: Alcoholism is a disease. At first, people drink to feel good, but some people become addicted. That means your body craves more and more just to feel OK. The body and brain must have the drug. When people try to withdraw from alcohol they can become very sick. This withdrawal can be mild, violent or fatal. Many people each year die from the effects of alcoholism which include: liver damage, brain damage, high blood pressure, and accidental death.

M: How can young people protect themselves from becoming alcoholic?

Dr. K: First, delay experimenting with alcohol until you are over 21. Second, avoid hanging out with people who experiment with drinking. And never, never, NEVER drive a car after drinking or accept a ride from someone else who has been drinking!

M: Thanks for the info, Dr. Knight! I think I'll stick to lemonade!

Thanks for the interview!

Dr. K: Wise choice, Maeve.

This is what happens to your body when you get drunk

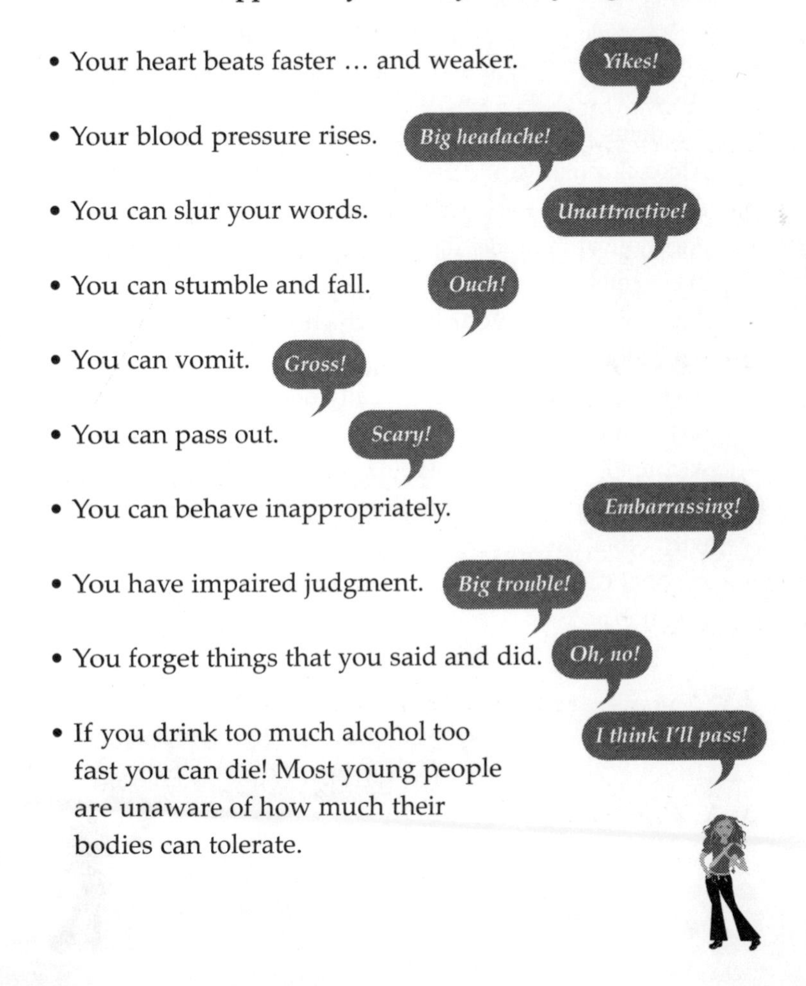

- Your heart beats faster … and weaker.
- Your blood pressure rises.
- You can slur your words.
- You can stumble and fall.
- You can vomit.
- You can pass out.
- You can behave inappropriately.
- You have impaired judgment.
- You forget things that you said and did.
- If you drink too much alcohol too fast you can die! Most young people are unaware of how much their bodies can tolerate.

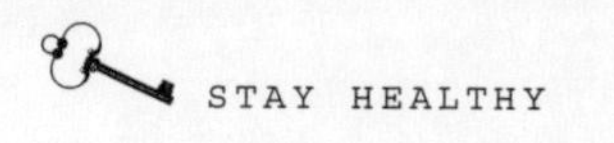

bodies can tolerate.

1. Alcohol can cause car crashes and other deadly accidents.
2. Alcohol makes some people become violent.
3. Alcohol can make good kids make really bad decisions.
4. Alcohol can damage the developing brain by killing off brain cells.
5. Alcohol can hurt your liver, which you need to clean your blood.
6. Alcohol can make you feel really depressed and sad, and even become suicidal.
7. Alcohol is illegal until you are 21 years old.
8. Young people who drink are more likely to experiment with other drugs.
9. Alcohol can lead to sexual assaults and unplanned pregnancy.

Check out www.the coolspot.gov for more info on teens and alcohol

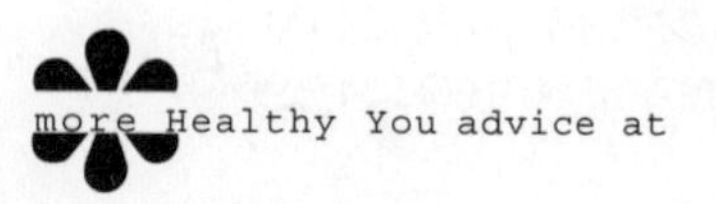

BSG

Join the BSG International Advisory Board

Be the first to find out about new books, products, contests, and special offers ✿

✿ Share your opinions with other BSG fans

Sign up now and get a free gift
(while supplies last)

Don't forget to visit www.beaconstreetgirls.com. We have games, quizzes, and a BSG shop!

Hey Girls!
Now you can
get all the
latest BSG
stuff!
BEACON STREET GIRLS
Pillows!
Books
Clutches
Bags
My favorite
Think Pink
bag!
BSG
our store is always open at:
www.beaconstreetgirls.com